Thomas Cooper De Leon

Crag-Nest

A Romance of the Days of Sheridan's Ride

Thomas Cooper De Leon

Crag-Nest
A Romance of the Days of Sheridan's Ride

ISBN/EAN: 9783337347826

Printed in Europe, USA, Canada, Australia, Japan

Cover: Foto ©Andreas Hilbeck / pixelio.de

More available books at **www.hansebooks.com**

CRAG-NEST.

A Romance of the Days of Sheridan's Ride.

By T. C. DeLEON,

Author of "Four Years in Rebel Capitals," "John Holden, Unionist," "Creole and Puritan," "The Puritan's Daughter," etc.

It is not the deeds that men do, so much as the manner of their doing, that set their impress upon an era.

MOBILE, ALA.
THE GOSSIP PRINTING CO.,
1897.

TO

THE MEMORY

OF MY LONG AND WELL-LOVED FRIEND,

Mrs. PRICE WILLIAMS, Jr.,

WHO WAS THE INSPIRATION OF ALL THAT WAS BEST IN

THE WIFE, MOTHER AND HOSTESS OF MY

"PURITAN'S DAUGHTER,"

I DEDICATE THIS BOOK.

CONTENTS.

INTRODUCTORY.

T HE pseudo-philosopher who said : " A book without a preface is a salad without salt," plainly valued his condiment above his comestible.

The latter-day story that does not tell itself, will gain little from the Greek " chorus" preceding it ; and, equally, he who can not read for himself does not want a book. Yet a word here may point merely the *raison d'etre* of this romance.

The war novel proper may be a trifle out of date ; one class of readers for it having largely passed away, while the other has not yet mellowed, by reading and thought, for its real enjoyment. But the present is scarcely a war novel proper, albeit its scenes concern themselves with the most active and stirring events of that most exceptional of wars — the struggle between the states.

The object of my " Four Years in Rebel Capitals " was not to write history ; only to give a truthful and familiar view of the gradual effect of the wearing strain and demoralization of civil war upon the tone and character of a people. But, in that book, very much had necessarily to be left unsaid ; even as in all war novels their story and movement force aside their yet more important idea. Even the graphic sketches of my gallant friend, John Esten Cooke, were given without pause to outline the result of the scenes he paints with virile and vivid brush.

It occurred to me that a romance of facts, and carrying with it their result — making result as it were the hero of the story — might bear more conviction than could either history, or story, separately. So I took a typical family of the Valley of Virginia and made its home seat, and its gradual changes, the feature of this tale. If I have drawn living men and women, they will do the task 1 set for myself ; for their surroundings are familiar ones to the time and the locality through which they move.

Portraiture has not been essayed ; though, of course, known people have typed the characters. Few who recall him will fail to see the lion-hearted, yet courtly, old colonel of the First Virginia in some phases of him a kindly critic christens "your Virginian Colonel Newcome ;" and the old Valley *grande dame* has a hundred prototypes in her own state.

Perchance, my particular Federal general never rode down the Valley

With light of burning roofs, to mark his course.

Still it is true that such wearers of the blue were not uncommon — as generous foes as they were gallant soldiers. Carping criticlings have said, ere this, that my novels : "Cater to Northern patronage, by making his Yankees heroes." Their shallowness babbled by this underlying truth : they detract from Southern heroism, who undervalue the men the South fought so long and so well.

All the Cavaliers did not ride south of the Potomac ; the grandest Puritan of the war had never seen Plymouth Rock.

With so much of preface, I leave this story to its readers. If its people be not of flesh and blood, then no words of mine could give it "pith and moment." If its results be not those of men's — and women's — acts, it will relegate itself to the Leporello-list of failures.

T. C. DeLeon.

Mobile, Ala., May 15, 1897.

CRAG-NEST.

A Romance of the Days of Sheridan's Ride.

CHAPTER I.

IN THE WINTER SIESTA.

Those were gay and reckless days of the early war!

The harsh hand of conflict had borne as yet but lightly upon the hearts of the people on either side of the Potomac; though there had been sufficient of the pomp and panoply of war to stir the prideful ambition of both sections. But its grim and ghastly realism—so well known later as to become an element of daily life—had not yet begun to irritate; far less to fester into hideousness.

Manassas had told its story of crude assault and dogged reception; a fight—like Chevy Chase, "of all a summer's day"—of green troops hurled against raw levies, resistless—perhaps intentless; of swirl, onset and blood, ending in wild rush for the Capital and timorous expectancy of that dread pursuit which never came.

Only came rest on arms, desultory watching

across the Potomac for weary months, as Manassas summer reddened into autumn; and that, in turn, whitened with early snows the mountain tops of the as yet untrampled Valley.

The first winter of the war may be regarded its moral cocktail; stimulant to expectation and tonic to hope, as precedent to that long orgy of blood, happily not yet set forth upon its *menu.*

In the early days of winter, a gay and thoughtless party of younger people assembled under the grave matronage of Mrs. Cabbell Courtenay in her Valley home. Crag-Nest, time out of mind the manor house of the Courtenays, had ever swung wide its hospitable doors; its widowed mistress clinging to traditions of her own race, and basing her life-habit on the memories of a husband, whose practice had ever been translation of the Arab's wordy proffer to his guest.

As the red glow of early sunset lingered about the brow of the mountain opposite, its reflection warmed the sloping lawn leading to the home; and the low, broad porch along which rapidly paced two young girls. Well dressed in latest style and fabric, these two presented, even to the casual glance, that marked contrast—in thought and manner, as well as appearance—which so often goes to cement girl friendships. Dark, ruddy and tall, Valerie Courtenay showed in every flash of her black eyes and every curve and

movement of her supple figure—in the very tread
of her slim boot and quick movement of the
slender, brown hand about her hairpins—the
conscious power, will and self reliance, foreign to
her fair companion. For Wythe Dandridge was
shorter by a head than her cousin and chosen con-
fidante; white, plump and soft, with peachblow
complexion and curves suggestive of dimple in
shoulder and elbow. Masses of soft, fair hair
coiled low upon her neck and shaded the low brow,
'neath which mild, blue eyes glanced furtively
toward the gate, as the pair halted at the door of
the sashed side porch that formed a conservatory.

Valerie Courtenay followed the other's glance
with a quick flash of her dark eyes as, with a mock
sigh, she quoted:

"'He cometh not,' she said, 'I am a-weary:' I
wonder if he's dead."

"Val!" was all Miss Dandridge replied. "How
can you?" But the real sigh came, as the soft
eyes again traveled to the gate.

"How can *he*," Val retorted demurely, "after
writing great oaths, that took eight portraits of
Mr. Davis to bring them through the mails, that
he would be here this very day. Much I fear, my
pretty coz, that he has surrendered, rescue or no
rescue, to that dreadful Baltimore girl; or else
has been captured *en route* by the flying artillery
belles at Winchester."

"You know you don't mean it, Val," Wythe Dandridge answered gravely. "And besides, why should *I* care? You know he wrote to you, not to me."

"*To* me and *for* you," Val answered saucily. "Why, my dear, I'm old enough to be his — aunt, if I am his cousin. I tell you, Wythe, he's a deserter."

"I'm sure he's detained by duty," the other pleaded seriously.

" 'The true knight's duty is to his ladye fayre;' and I am sure — "

"Listen!—horses' feet!" the fairer girl broke in, bending her little pink shell of an ear toward the yet faint sounds. "It must be he!"

"Undoubtedly," Val assented, leaning calmly against the pillar, "for there is no other rider in the Valley; and Master Rob Maury always rides four-in-hand."

"There *are* several horses," the other girl answered; still listening eagerly and with heightened color. "They are coming so fast. Oh! I hope nothing has happened!"

"Nothing more serious I warrant," Miss Courtenay answered, "than a squad bringing news of his being shot for desertion; or perhaps Master Rob is bringing in some Yankee picket that captured him. Don't you think so, aunt?"

"What a rattlebrain you are, Val," the lady

addressed replied. She stepped from the conservatory and carefully closed the sashed doors
with firm, white, patrician hands, on which the
lined, blue veins alone spoke of great age. Taller
than either girl, with the grace of belleship from
another age showing in every pose and in every
fold of her severely made black silk gown, Mrs.
Courtenay looked a perfect portrait of colonial
days, just stepped from its frame. The clear,
white skin, softened still more by hair of spun
silver, pompadoured high back from the broad
brow; the aquiline nose, full but firm lips and
partly doubled chin gave singular strength to a
face in which benevolence blended with power,
only to be dominated at times by the steady gleam
of steel gray eyes, undimmed by age and unyield-
ing to the modern fad for "glasses." Calm, self-
reliant simplicity spoke in every line of face and
figure and dress; its crowning the stiff and towering back of her widow's cap, of which the frill and
strings hung loose behind her coronet of hair. No
gleam of jewel, chain or ring relieved severe simplicity of dress, save only the heavy circlet of gold
about her wedding finger.

"Visitors, aunt; and several of them," Val
said, as the clatter of hoofs grew clear and sharp
on the hard mountain road and a party of four
horsemen, at a rapid trot, swung round the curve
of the hill and bore down upon the gate.

"They are ever welcome," Mrs. Courtenay replied—one of her rare smiles showing even, white teeth, of nature's making. "They are doubly so when they wear our uniform. But see, my children! That taller horseman is our cousin, Wirt." And the lady of the manor moved toward the broad steps, as the riders clattered through the gate and up the path.

"And the tall young rider behind him is our cousin, Rob Maury," Val whispered to her cousin, as she followed her aunt.

"And the other is Lieutenant Caskie Cullen," Wythe Dandridge whispered back; a most unnecessary blush tinting her soft cheek and what of her neck peeped above her collar.

Erect, stern and soldierly, the elder officer rode up; drawing rein as he lifted his corded hat and gravely bent his broad shoulders; then swinging from saddle with the easy grace of a young horseman. Over six feet of height seemed even more from length of sinewy limb and lank, muscular body; its depth of rounded chest denoting unusual strength. The close fitting shell-jacket and buff riding pants answered to play of muscle; the high riding boots ended in slim, high-arched feet; while the ungauntleted hand that raised his hat was firm and white, but nervous as if gripping the hilt of his famous sword. For few men in the Army of Virginia could draw that blade from scabbard

with one sweep, so great was its keen and shining
length.

Every inch the cavalier looked Colonel Wirt
Calvert, as well he might with the bluest blood of
sister states coursing through his veins. Straight
descended through his sire from the first lords of
Maryland, his mother's forbears had early landed
at Jamestown. And upon the face that fitly top-
ped his stalwart frame, the marks of descent and
personality were traced with equal clearness.
The high, sloping forehead, its temples fringed
sparsely with snow-white hair; the deep-set blue
eyes beneath heavy gray brows; the firm-based
nose with ample nostrils, and the long-sloped jaw
with full, beardless chin, denoted tenacity of the
"Island Mastiff," tempered by high intelligence.
But that tell-tale feature, the mouth, spoke no
further clue to the complex machinery within; for
the long sweep of a huge, gray mustache completely veiled it and curved about the jaw. So, as he
tossed his rein to the ready orderly, never moving
the blue eyes from the ladies, as he advanced with
bared head, Colonel Calvert seemed best exemplar
of those "Golden Horse Shoe Knights," whom the
Southern poet wrote:

> "The knightliest of the knightly race,
> Who, since the days of old,
> Have kept the lamp of chivalry
> Alight in hearts of gold—

The kindliest of the kindly band
  Who rarely hated ease,
Who rode with Smith around the land,
  And Raleigh round the seas!

"Who climbed the blue Virginia hills
  Amid embattled foes,
And planted there, in valleys fair,
  The lily and the rose—
Whose fragrance lives in many lands,
  Whose beauty stars the earth,
And lights the hearths of many homes
  With loveliness and worth!"

Educated at St. Cyr, with the cadets of a noble French family—whose head had fought by Major Herbert Calvert's side in Washington's campaigns and had shared his blanket at Valley Forge—the son added the softer graces of Parisian manner to the more solid courtliness of the old school Virginian.

"We were fortunate indeed, Cousin Virginia," he said, with a bow a marshal of the Empire might have given before Josephine, "that our duty and pleasure unite in laying our road to your door. Thrice fortunate—" he added as he raised his head, after touching his mustache to the extended hand of his kinswoman, and his keen glance rested kindly on the two girls—"in finding your fair young aides on duty."

And the tall head bent not so low this time, as

the grim mustache swept lightly each fresh forehead:

"Why, my little cousins, you grow prettier
every time we meet! But, pardon, Cousin Virginia! You know my young friend, Maury; let
me present Lieutenant Fraser Ravanel, of Charleston."

"You were ever welcome, sir," the old lady said
gently, "simply as a Carolina soldier; more so as
my kinsman's friend. But you have a higher
claim to command me and mine if, as I believe,
your mother was Sarah Routlege, my schoolmate
at Philadelphia. My nieces, Miss Courtenay—
Miss Dandridge,—Mr. Ravanel."

Robert Maury, boyish, agile and gay, had
thrown himself from his horse and was already
shaking hands heartily with both girls; but Wythe
Dandridge's blue eyes looked beyond the young
soldier, to open wide with surprise at the deeper
crimson disc that jumped into Val Courtenay's
pleasure-flushed cheek, as her eyes meet the grave,
gray ones of the tall Carolina cavalryman. But
he advanced with lazy grace, taking the old lady's
hand courteously, as he said in his soft, seaboard
accent:

"You are so good to remember her, Mrs. Courtenay! I have often heard ma speak of her school-
days; and I must compliment her by saying that
she is as well preserved as yourself. I am

2

charmed to meet Miss Dandridge, after hearing
so much of her,"—he again bowed suavely;
adding easily—"and Miss Courtenay and I are
scarcely strangers."

"Oh! how delightful—" Wythe began aloud to
Rob Maury; but the other girl broke in a trifle
rapidly, the color still lingering in her face:

"Yes, aunt; Mr. Ravanel and I have met at
Judge Brooke's, in Richmond. But, Cousin Wirt,
how does it chance that you all came this way;
adding"—she finished with her old manner and a
quick glance at Miss Dandridge—"so much to all
our pleasure?"

"Providence and the War Department," the
veteran answered. "I have been transferred to
command of the —th Cavalry; and our base of
operations will be the Valley for the present."

"Oh! I'm so glad!" chirped Miss Dandridge.

"So am I," echoed Rob Maury.

"I may venture to join the chorus?" the Carolinian said quietly. But the interrogation point
was made by the flash of his gray eyes, as they
met the dark ones Val Courtenay chanced to lift
at his words.

CHAPTER II.

THE OLD VIRGINIA HOME.

Crag-Nest loked little warlike, as the family and its guests sat about the old-time table, loaded with triumphs of the Virginian *cuisine*. Sturdy men of war—their appetites sharpened by brisk riding through crisp, mountain air, and their viands sauced by warmest welcome and charming companionship—charged valorous upon the ramparts of fried chicken and swept resistless over barricades of raised biscuits. They decimated long ranks of brown muffins and the pig-ham melted as they bore down like the Guard at Waterloo. Amber coffee flowed free, and now—the main onset done—they pressed no less vigorously the rear-guard of airy waffles and flannel cakes, of which the flankers were literally "flowing with milk and honey." But in the pauses of pleasant conflict, the colonel had told his story, not unaided by volunteer aidship of Master Robert Maury, who stopped low-toned prattle with Val Courtenay to throw out interjectory comment, endorsement, or approval.

The —th Cavalry was a crack regiment of noted riders, with history-noted names; and its selection for outpost and scout duty followed the promotion of its colonel to a western brigade. Unsought, and through fitness only, came Colonel Calvert's transfer from infantry to the more congenial service; his perfect knowledge of the Valley and its people pointing to him as the man for that post.

"My headquarters will not be far away, Cousin Virginia; and I need not add that you and your fair aides will be ever welcome on your visits of inspection. The regiment is marching there; but we spurred ahead—"

"So plainly to our advantage, sir," Rob put in, his mouth rather too full of waffle and honey. "The colonel has made me his courier, Cousin Val; and from now on I'll look down from a McClellan tree on these poor infantry tramps."

"I promised your father to make a man of you, when he fell into my arms at Cerro Gordo, Rob," the old man said with gentler voice; adding, as he brushed back the flowing gray mustache: "And I'll do it, if you ever grow out of being a big boy!"

"And you are with the —th Cavalry, also?" Mrs. Courtenay turned graciously to her stranger guest, who had sat quietly through the meal, taking small part in the current of talk.

"Temporarily, I am on special duty, ma'am," he answered; adding quickly: "On detail for engineer duty. But I had no idea of being first ordered on such pleasant special service as this."

"Your mother's son must ever be a welcome

guest at Crag-Nest," the old lady replied with a smile. "Cousin Wirt puts me under compliment by permitting me to entertain you, even for the brief two days."

But the man's eyes had again caught Miss Courtenay's and some restraint and absence showed in his perfunctory:

"You are too good, ma'am!"

"And of course you dance, Captain Ravanel?" Miss Dandridge exclaimed. "You must; riding so well as you do!" Then, catching Rob's wide stare fixed on her, the younger girl blushed rosily at her implied confession of prompt study of the stranger's points, as she corrected herself:—"As Mr. Maury says you do."

"Did I say that?" Rob blurted out, boy fashion. "I don't remember it, but it's true though. I'm no bad horseman myself, but I reckon Mr. Ravanel can give me points."

"I have been riding longer than he has, Miss Dandridge," Ravanel said with a smile that showed white teeth under his drooping mustache —"You ride, of course?"

"Oh! I dote on it," the girl cried naively; "but I don't ride like Val—"

"I have been riding longer than she has," Miss Courtenay finished for her. And again her eyes met the man's; this time not dropping under them, though the color deepened in her oval cheeks.

"I am glad you do," he continued quietly to Wythe; not even answering her cousin's look. "I have a very clever, well-gaited mare with the wagons, and I hope you will permit me to offer her and myself for your service, Miss Dandridge."

"Aunt Virginia is very careful about Miss Wythe's mounts," Rob Maury put in abruptly—"Your mare is a little fresh sometimes, Mr. Ravanel."

"All young animals are apt to be, on occasion," the Carolinian responded quietly. "But, like her master, Santee yields naturally to feminine hand. You will permit me"—he turned courteously to his hostess—"when I have become less of a stranger?"

"But you haven't answered if you dance," Wythe persisted, "and I'm just sure you do!"

The man's eyes, absently gazing through the wide window on the crescent moon just cresting the distant mountain, never changed as he answered half to himself:

"I used to—it seems so long ago!"

And the far away look deepened in the eyes that, had he turned them, might have seen Val Courtenay's as well travel to the distant mountain top, while the same far away look deepened in them and her aunt spoke twice ere she recalled herself with a little start.

"I beg pardon, aunt. Yes, Cousin Wirt, it will

be delightful; and the War Department builded wiser than it knew when it sent us protectors, partners, horses and proffers of picnics, all in one."

"We should celebrate their advent," Wythe Dandridge cried with a merry laugh.

"And so you shall, my dears," Mrs. Courtenay assented cheerily. "As soon as the —th regiment pitches its tents you shall have a dance of welcome"—she bowed gravely to the colonel—"if its commander permits."

"On one condition solely"—the veteran answered—"that my kinswoman walks the polonaise with me. Jove! I have not danced one since that night in Paris when the Marquis feted the Russian Crown Princess. I was a slim youth then, Cousin Virginia,"—he went on, waxing reminiscent—"but I remember my lavender silk stockings and silver buckles; and how Madame la Marquise honored the young American by giving him her hand."

"Was she pretty, sir?" Rob Maury queried with his now empty mouth half open, as if to gulp in the answer.

"She was a grand lady, sir, with the blood of princes in her veins," the colonel responded with slight frown; but turning to his kinswoman: "A great man, the Marquis, Cousin Virginia, in peace as in war. Jove! it was he first taught my father the true secret of *filet de truite, a la sauce Tartare!*"

And the veteran pronounced the last word with a fatness of rolled r's and an Epicurean gurgle that would have made Brillat Savarin proud to hear. "Those were rare days, when I hobnobbed with royal descendants!"

"It was your right of birth, Cousin Wirt," the old lady said mildly, but raising her full chin proudly. "The blood of the Calverts and Cabbells is the peer of any king's! So, as a daughter of their house, I accept my kinsman's invitation and will succeed Madame la Marquise in the polonaise. —But I am forgetting, my kinsman, that all our guests have ridden hard to-day." She rose from her seat, bowing courteously to all in signal. "Ezekiel! The gentlemen's candles!—Good-night and pleasant dreams to all. As we are not on duty, we will breakfast at eight."

The statue of shining ebony standing by the ponderous, carved sideboard and reflecting in its polished silverware vast wealth of shirt front and standing collar above his blue dress coat, waved stately right hand to the door and swayed his long back with haughty bend, as he proclaimed:

"Da gennelmun's can'ls am served!"

The two girls stood a moment silent, after the matron's gentle good-night kiss upon their foreheads; Val Courtenay's eyes fixed steadily upon the now high-riding moon, her companion's staring straight ahead at nothing, as the blood stole redder to her cheek. Then she woke with a little sigh and exclaimed:

"Oh! Val, isn't he nice?"

Miss Courtenay came back slowly from the mountain top, as she answered rather wearily:

"Oh, yes, he's a nice enough boy——"

"Boy! Why Val, he must be thirty if he's a day! And so you have met him before?"

"Oh! I thought you referred to my cousin," the other girl answered quietly. "Yes, I met Mr. Ravanel in Richmond—casually—when I staid with Coulter Brooke."

"You didn't like him much," Wythe persisted naively. "You didn't seem a bit glad to see him."

"You did; and plainly told him so," the elder girl answered rather tartly. "No, don't pout, dear; but you know I never gush over"—she hesitated a moment, then slowly dropped the words—"men I don't know. But it will be very nice to have Rob so near, and useful as a walking stick and riding beau."

"Yes, Rob is very nice," Miss Dandridge replied, again looking across the room at nothing. "But one might wish that he had a little more style."

"There are better things than style, Wythe," Val answered seriously; some surprise creeping into the eyes she fixed upon her cousin. "Rob Maury is a gentleman in birth and in heart. When you have been in society as long as I have, you will learn that these are born, and unlike style, can not be made. But come, dear, we're to breakfast at eight and 'da ladies can'ls am served.'" She passed her arm gently around the fair, plump shoulders and bending down pressed a genuine kiss upon the pouting lips. Then the girls lit the tapers in the grand old silver sticks on the sideboard and softly passed up the broad, oak stairway to the upper hall, across which came, in regular volleys, sounds most unlike that of

"The horns of elfland faintly blowing,"

suggesting that Colonel Wirt Calvert might be dreaming of too much *filet de truite a la sauce Tartare*.

CHAPTER III.

BY THE "DAUGHTER OF THE STARS."

The regiment had arrived, gone into comfortable winter quarters and settled down to routine of camp duty.   But two days had been needed for its officers to learn the road to Crag-Nest, where senior and sub alike shared the boundless hospitality of the lady of the manor, and the latter especially had been welcomed warmly by the young girls. Already there had been a riding party to the river; Miss Dandridge mounted on "Santee," with her master as attendant cavalier, while Val Courtenay rode her own fiery chestnut beside Master Robert Maury's eager and restless bay.

The always bright-tempered girl had been in unusual flow of spirits these two days; caused, as Wythe hinted to her, by nearness of new scalps, possible of affixment to her slim girdle; and on this ride she grew almost reckless. Gully and stream seemed nothing to her mettlesome horse; and more than once she turned out of the road to put him at a fence stiff enough to test the best powers of her escort's mount. And after one of these, as they galloped in chase of the pair ahead, the boy suddenly said:

"Odd, Cousin Val; but *you* don't seem to like him.—And women always do, too!"

"So I have —" the girl checked the involuntary exclamation; nodding toward the couple ahead, as she finished with a laugh—"begun to imagine, Rob. You must watch your 'Lily maid' or she will be broidering stranger Launcelot's shield, ere he rides away."

"Pshaw! You don't mean it, Cousin Val!" the boy blurted out, as a hot flush crossed his face. "She doesn't come of a kind that are won without wooing—"

"As you know, Sir Laggard!" she broke in merrily.

"And the man's a perfect stranger," he went on glumly. "But he's a deuced handsome and dashing one, too; and he's such a perfect gentleman!"

"Is he?" For a second the girl's dark eyes lost their merry gleam; a bitter ring in her voice. Then her laugh chimed out again, as she added:

"And he's so fond of his—'ma'!"

"Yes, he is," Master Rob assented loyally. "*You* don't think less of him for devotion to his family, Cousin Val? And it's a good one, too. I'm not much gone on Mr. Ravanel, for he's too cold and proud to suit my book, and he thinks privates no better than rice-field niggers. But he's

a man and a brave one, and a good soldier for all
that. By Jove! how he rides!"

The officer's black, chafing and lurching side-
ways under the strong bridle hand, suddenly
snorted and reared almost upright. But the
quick feet left the stirrups, the knees gripped the
saddle closer and the man threw his weight forward, as the corded neck went straight up. And
with the one motion the heavy gauntlet in the
bare right hand crashed down between the horse's
ears. Even as the blow fell, the clear soft-toned
voice said, with the same drawing-room accent:

"Pull to the left, Miss Dandridge! Santee may
fret."

The black was down again; chafing under
punishment of the spur, but obedient to the seeming light hand on the curb; and Wythe Dandridge,
her glowing cheeks and frank eyes speaking ad-
miration, loosened the mare's head and bowled
along confidently by her escort. Profile, pose and
rapid speech, unheard across distance, told plainly
that she was complimenting him, and again the
older girl's eyes darkened strangely, and the line
of her full lips grew straighter from their pressure
together. Then she answered lightly:

"A very Lochinvar, come out of the——South!
Beware, Master Laggard, lest he mount our 'fair
Ellen' upon his horse's croup and ride away from
us all!"

She gave the chestnut his head and sped away after the others to the turn of the road that showed the Shenandoah just ahead. High beyond, the Massanutten reared his towering forehead; haloed now by golden reflection from the sunset; while trending southward the lower crests of Three Top mountain began to lose their profiles in the evening shadow. Just at their feet the "Daughter of the Stars" * bared her broad, smooth bosom to the reflected glow, as though ready for the coming gleam of her myriad-eyed mother.

The quartette drew rein, descending to the bank; Val Courtenay's eyes bent steadily upon the fast rippling stream; her escort's fixed furtively upon the fair, flushed face of the other girl. Gradually the restless mare moved upward along the bank, and gradually—obeying imperceptible turn of Maury's wrist—the restless bay kept even pace with her. But, as he sat statue-like in his saddle, Ravanel's gaze followed Miss Courtenay's toward the stream, whether or not it went beyond herself. Suddenly and with a half start, Val came back to the present; her eyes turned toward her missing cousins, who had disappeared around the turn of the bank—then resting in surprise upon her sole companion. He too came back to himself; and, all society man at once, he moved the black up abreast the chestnut.

---

* Literal translation of the Indian name, Shenandoah.

"I fear it has seemed a little like intrusion, Miss Courtenay;" he said quietly, raising his hat, "but my presence under your roof was the fault of circumstances rather than myself."

"As my aunt's guest," she replied coldly—all her interest again seeming to center on the river—"*I* have no possible right to criticise. As her kinsman's friend, you were doubtless entirely welcome"—there was almost imperceptible pause ere she finished—"to her."

"I think I have the right," the man said gravely, ignoring her equivoke, "to ask one question. What was your ground for deciding that we should be strangers?"

"Was it not sufficient that I so decided?" was the girl's answer calmly given.

"No! Assuredly not," he retorted earnestly but quietly. "Even the law grants the accused the right to hear the charge against him and to plead in his own defense. When a man is condemned unheard by the lady who has said——"

"What she prefers not to remember, her wish should be the only law to——," again she made the least perceptible pause—"the gentleman."

Fraser Ravanel looked steadily at the half averted face while he might have counted thirty; no perceptible change showing itself on his own. Then he said in low, even voice:

"I have always thought myself a man—I have

believed you a woman, Valerie Courtenay. So I speak to you now; not as society gentleman to lady. When we parted that night in Richmond; when I had asked for, and you had granted a pledge——"

"Which I have said I would forget," she broke in, her voice quivering, her eyes darkening upon the river.

"——Which you had taught me to expect; and to which I claim I have forfeited no right," he went on, ignoring the interruption, "I was cast aside as a used glove; my letters first unanswered, then returned unopened! Should not justice, if not courtesy, grant me an explanation?"

"To what avail?" she queried, her face still averted; the bosom of her close fitting habit rising and falling rapidly.

"That I may clear myself of unjust suspicion," the man answered firmly. "When one who has ever kept faith with man and woman gives his solemn pledge——"

"He should keep it for at least an hour, Mr. Ravanel!" Her face turned full to him; her eyes steadily meeting his that never fell before their searching accusation, although some wonderment rose into them.

"I am waiting." His voice was not raised or changed. "Please go on; you can not deny my right to be curious, now."

"You can not deny my right to act as I did,"

she answered rapidly, "if you have memory enough
to recall that night at the station."

"I recall every instant of it," he said very gently;
"how you looked and spoke at the ball; how you
were good enough to dance but once; how I pledged
my word never to dance again, until I might with
you; how we left the crowded room for the conservatory; how I there spoke words that——"

"Had far better been left unsaid." She sat
erect in saddle; her cheeks burning, with her eyes
still fixed bravely on his.

"Perhaps," he answered low but firmly; "but I
must first ask you to prove that, as far as I am
concerned."

"What need?" she answered more hotly; the
swell of her bosom more rapid. "I retained my
eyesight that night, even if you lost your memory.
But we are in the mountains, and we are playing
at society. Let us end the comedy and rejoin my
cousins."

As she spoke she turned her horse's head
quickly; but with equal swiftness the black barred
her way.

"One moment first," the man said gravely. "It
is no comedy to me; nor are the scenes of my making. But you, Valerie Courtenay, were the first
woman to whom I ever spoke serious word of love;
you make yourself the first lady whose command
I have disobeyed. No man of my race has ever

3

proved disloyal to his plighted word. I were disloyal to them and to myself, did I not demand something more definite than this merely hinted charge!"

The girl's lip curled and her voice was hard that scoffed:

"Really, sir, you are a better actor than I had suspected."

"Possibly," he answered quietly, but more rapidly, "for I feel as I act. I am no child; you no woman to speak lightly such words as you once said to me. Why should we throw away what might be precious to us both, when a single word from you might clear up a hideous mistake that comes between us? Valerie! Through all these many months; through silence, even contempt, I have never doubted you. No! do not speak! *Had* I, my self respect had never let me allude to the past, far less plead for the future, as I do now."

Once more the girl's eyes fell before his earnest gaze, resting on—if not seeing—the far rolling river. Once more the rapid movement of her bosom spoke the hot tumult within; but the full lips pressed firmly together, and the clinch of her hand upon the rein bore her spirited horse some paces backward. But she spoke no word; and again the man—low and rapidly, and with something like pity in his voice—said:

"Do not be afraid to speak! Anything is better

than this silence; anything more just to me and to
—yourself!"

"What need?" the voice was scarcely hers in
its tremulous hardness; "you must remember that
night!"

"I have told you I do," he answered. "When
you left the ball room, I said I would see you at
the train. There I slipped the rosebud into the
little hand that spoke farewell so loyally; the
train that bore you from me moved rapidly away,
but left me full of joy and hope."

The girl's lips quivered as she still looked at the
river. Two deep red spots rose to her cheeks and
something like a sob seemed to rise into her throat;
but she bravely conquered herself, saying only:

"Was that all?"

"That was all," he answered firmly, "save that
you went from me, either to sport with, or
strangely to misjudge me. If I speak falsely, by
your truth to your own womanhood, I demand that
you prove it!"

A changed woman turned in that saddle; her
form erected and her glowing eyes fixed upon his
with glance as proud and stern as his own. The
red had gone from her face, but left it firm as
pale, as with steady voice she answered:

"I have sought, honestly, to avoid this explanation and yourself equally. You taunt me with
injustice; and demand, by my honor and self

respect, the brutality of words! Very well; you shall have them. That train you saw whirl me away, soon backed swiftly into the depot, opposite. From its window, a chance glance showed me an incoming train. From it stepped a—lady. A gentleman scanning the train approached eagerly. There was surprised recognition—joyous greeting. An instant, and her head was on his shoulder—his arms about her!"

Pale, with compressed lips and brows contracted, over eyes that gleamed back almost fiercely into hers, Fraser Ravanel sat motionless in his saddle, with never a word of reply. So, for what might have been many seconds. Then the man, all himself once more, backed his horse from her path as he lifted his hat with graceful sweep and said in his soft, drawing-room voice:

"We will hunt for your cousins, Miss Courtenay."

CHAPTER IV.

A BIT OF SAGE ADVICE.

The ball to welcome its new military neighbors was in mid revel at Crag-Nest. The house had been so arranged as to give the most space possible to the dancers; tightly drawn tent flies, draped with borrowed flags, enclosed the wide verandah and formed a cosy supper room, where a buffet, amply filled with solids and sweets, and majestically presided over by Ezekiel, in even more ample show of linen, tempted old and young in intervals of talk or dance. The glassed conservatory—Mrs. Courtenay's pride and solace, in those intervals when her hospitality took vacation from very lack of material on which to lavish it—opened inviting doors upon this improvised supper room; and its cool walks, bordered with tall, tubbed garden plants and some rare exotics, lit by softened gleam of swinging lamps, enticed more than one waltz-wearied couple to seductive seats in shadowed corners.

Colonel Calvert had walked "the opening polonaise" of the *fete* with his stately kinswoman; her severe black costume relieved for the occasion by soft falls of rare old lace, unique of design and time-shaded from amber to rich coffee color. And

a gracious pair they showed, those relics of the
good old times; merry, calm and grand, through
their rhythmic walk, with best adherence to time
permissible under coercion of an improvised or-
chestra—two fiddles, flute and guitar.   Grave,
watchful and yet with nearer approach to tremor
than ever hostile charge had brought him, the
colonel led the dance; his step measured, his head
erect above the deep, inflated chest; and his bows
perfection.   And his partner's pace was measured
stateliness, equal to his own; serene pleasure
seated upon her strongly marked features, now
softly flushed with pleasurable thought of joy to
others at her bidding.   Then—the polonaise completed and the lancers danced, "just to break the
ice, you know," as Rob Maury explained—the
negro fiddlers struck up a rattling waltz and eager
beaux sought no unwilling partners.   Gray shell-
jackets, orange trimmed and yet unsmirched with
powder and camp smoke, contrasted prettily with
soft dresses of the girls; for, so early in the war no
scarcity was felt, even in matter of dress, and the
guests embraced the whole higher population of
the lower Valley accessible to call.   Fair faces and
graceful forms showed on every hand; the varying
types proclaiming descent from many a different
stock; but—brunette or blonde, matron or maid—
each woman present showed the ease of access to
"the best society," and the nameless charm of

gentle breeding gave a tone to the whole affair, too
often missing in more ambitious congregations of
some great city's "leaders." Nor were the men
lacking in that courtliness and deference to sex,
typical of old Virginian days. The undecorated
jacket of the beardless youth, the star-decked coat
of the chevroned officer, alike covered the best
blood of the Old Dominion; for the —th Cavalry
was truly a *corps d'elite*, and sire and son of that
day made practical the idea of the German poet:

> Honor to woman! To her it is given
> To garland the earth with the roses of heaven!

Waltz, quadrille and lancers had succeeded
each other, soft speech from bearded lips had
brought the pleasure-flush to delicate cheeks;
and already the polished, bald forehead of Ezekiel and his household staff gleamed with shinier
ebon, from the moisture of grateful exercise. But
"the labor we delight in physics pain;" and the
butler of Crag-Nest grew less stately—indeed almost condescended to graciousness—under con-
sciousness of pleasure-giving, as viceroy of that
house's head.

"One shabin' ov da ham, Morse Wirt!" he plead,
holding back the plate for which the veteran extended his hand. "Miss 'Ginia raised da pig, sah;
an' I'be seed to de curin' mysef! Jess a shabin',
sah; ter gib da ellerment fur da bone-tukkey."

A dexterous twist of the slim, keen carver curled the rich, red meat across its back as the negro spoke; and he extended the plate with a bow in which grandeur and gratified pride bore equal part.

"Yes, Cousin Virginia," the colonel went on—not forgetting his grave bow of acknowledgment as he took the plate, "I repeat that no home in the Valley—I might add, in all our state—can equal Crag-Nest for its combination of home-comfort, old-school courtliness and generosity of welcome. Why, were poor Courtenay looking down upon us now, even that prince of entertainers could ask no addition to this scene. It makes me young again! It makes me prouder of my boys, to see that they need as little disciplining for the parlor as they do for the field. Jove! I would not scruple to order a chance detail from the —th to fall out, and carry them to a soirée at the Marquis' palace, without a word of warning!"

"You are right, kinsman," the hostess replied with a half sigh. "I have heard slurs upon us for our state-love and for our assumed superiority. But is it assumed, or actual? Look over these youths—boys, some of them; and tell me if the mothers of any state send more precious 'food for powder', or send more bravely and willingly, for duty's sake!"

"None!" he answered sonorously, with swift

sweep aside of his mustache. "In this home-brewed punch I drink to these mothers of noble sons. Scoffers call our state the mother of presidents. Jove! they will learn to respect her as the mother of soldiers!"

A gleam of sadness swept across the matron's face, glowing responsive to his words, as she answered:

"Never before have I so regretted, cousin, that there was no heir to Crag-Nest! And yet, what horrid gaps this war may make in all Virginia homes. Think of the mourning left from Manassas!"

"*Dulce et decorum!*" the soldier quoted gravely, setting down his emptied glass, not without a little smack of the mustache-hidden lips. "Bellona is the twin of sireless Mors, Cousin Virginia. Revolutions are not made with rose water; and this one is against a race akin to us; as staunch and stubborn as ourselves—although we have the right to fight for. Some of these youngsters will drop out of our ranks—many a one will leave his legacy of sorrow and tears behind; but each will leave also his legacy of glory for his own name, and of incentive to his comrades who remain! They *are* a splendid set of fellows! Jove! I do not believe any Washington soiree could equal their natural ease and elegance. My old comrades at St. Cyr had equal outside polish; they never

equaled those inner graces of head and heart,
born with these boys of mine!"

"There is the most *distingue* man present," Mrs.
Courtenay answered; adding with half regret, half
wonder:—"And he is not a Virginian."

"He is first cousin to it," her kinsman replied,
with a thoughtful twist of his mustache tips.
"South Carolina is most like us, of all the Confederacy; only she is a trifle hide-bound and be-
lieves no state equal to her. A good fault for a
soldier-producing country, cousin. And, besides,
Fraser Ravanel was educated in France, at *L' Ecole
Polytechnique.*"

"And he seems to admire Wythe very much,"
the lady retorted, more gravely than relevantly.

"Jove! I should order a court of inquiry on
him if he did not," the veteran answered with a
smile. "And now, Ezekiel, just another scrap of
that chicken-salad and a shaving of ham!"

"Oh! Cousin Wirt, isn't this just too nice a
dance?" Wythe Dandridge cried as she came up
radiant, flushed and leaning on Mr. Ravanel's gold-
embellished sleeve. "But I must have some
lemonade. Give me a glass, Uncle Ziek; quick, for
I'm *so* thirsty."

"Try this punch, my dear," the colonel answered, handing her a brimming glass. "Lemon,
rum, tea, cognac and champagne; the very Regent's
receipt the Marquis gave my father, the year I was

born!" And Sir Charles Grandison had made no
grander bow than that the veteran bent over the
thin glass proffered to the young girl.

"Your home is perfection, for entertaining, Mrs
Courtenay," Ravanel said easily. "Ma is very
proud of her wide rooms, overlooking the Battery,
with Charleston harbor stretching away to the
ocean. But, to us from the lowlands, the grand
old mountains out there are even grander; and this
glorious air is a real tonic."

"I rejoice that you like the Valley, sir," the old
lady replied half absently; "but I remember how
lonely your mother must be, in her seaside home,
if you are her only child."

For an instant only, the man stood mute; then,
flushing hotly, he answered rapidly:

"Yes, ma'am; I am my mother's only child!"

And Val Courtenay, leaning upon a burly
major's arm, passed near enough to catch the
words, and answer rather at random to her escort's
glowing compliment, as her aunt waved her fan
with old school grace as accent to her words:

"And I can realize how justly proud she must
be of you, sir."

But the girl's face grew dark and stern, and
her eyes—dropped on the floor—had an evil gleam
in them, as the old lady's praise fell upon her ear.
And the blood surged tingling toward her brain,
as the bright supper room changed for her to a

dingy, smoke filled railway station; and memory's camera held up the bold negative of a pale faced girl, crushing a white rose in her clinched hand, as she saw a tall, graceful man bend his head and press the lips of the eager-seeming woman clasped in his arms! And, as she raised her eyes, Val Courtenay felt that man's full upon them; while Wythe Dandridge, refreshed by the colonel's prescription, cried to her:

"Oh! Val, *isn't* it too nice? And Mr. Ravanel declares he doesn't dance well! *You* know if he used to; and I'm *sure* he must!"

Herself in a moment, the older girl slammed memory's camera close shut; the man before her was an every day acquaintance at once, and her voice wholly indifferent as she answered:

"I believe Mr. Ravanel was considered the best dancer in Richmond."

"Which reminds me that I should claim you quickly, Miss Dandridge, before his prowess captures my waltz with you," the burly major broke in. And next instant the young girl—her hand slipped into the speaker's arm, as she moved toward the dancing room—turned a glowing face over her shoulder and cried:

"Oh, Val! *make* him dance again, then! You can have the second from this, Mr. Ravanel."

Only the four stood near the buffet; the colonel and the hostess facing them; Val Courtenay and her dismissed lover facing each other with perfect nonchalance in seeming, but wary watch in either's eyes, as in the trained fencer's. A second's silence; then Ravanel's voice fell soft and low upon the girl's ear:

"I were indeed recreant knight did I refuse to lift that gage, Miss Courtenay," he said. "Will you risk my want of practice, and dance with me?"

Never hesitating one instant, but with closer pressure of her lips and slight paling of her exercise-flushed cheeks, Val Courtenay answered slowly:

"I do not fear your—want of practice, Mr. Ravanel."

"And you will dance?" he cried more eagerly.

"I am under my own roof; you are my aunt's guest," she replied, so low that only the man caught the words, as she turned from the others and let her fingers barely touch the arm he had proffered as eagerly as he spoke. "As her representative, *I* should regret an ungracious act, even did inclination prompt it."

He halted an instant. Then his lips set tight under their drooping black fringe, and he moved on again toward the music. Neither spoke word more as his arm passed about her slim waist and the pair glided out amid the dancers. One brief turn, and the burly major swung Wythe full against the

graceful moving pair; even the Carolinian's strong
arm and dexterous guidance failing to avert col-
lision.   But as they recovered poise, Val Courtenay stood free of his encircling arm, smiling
quietly at the major's warm excuses; while Wythe,
her eyes dancing and her cheeks aglow, was crying:

"Oh! aren't you ashamed, Mr. Ravanel? You
do dance as well as you ride!"

"That's saying a great deal, Miss Wythe!" Rob
Maury puffed out, as he ran up mopping his brow.
"May I have a turn?"

But Wythe's blue eyes were still upon the other
man's and, his making the query suggested by his
words, he answered for her:

"I believe Miss Dandridge promised me."

Only a nod at Rob was her reply; her hand
upon the Carolinian's shoulder and her little feet
flying in time to those of the best partner she had
ever met.   And Val Courtenay's eyes moved from
the fair, joyous face to the dark, stern-set one, with
the pity in them changing to angry contempt as
she caught his almost whisper:

"*I* have kept my pledge!"

"And may I hope, Miss Courtenay—," the
major began.   But Val—coming back to society
in view of impending martyrdom—smiled sweetly
on him as she put her hand on Rob Maury's
shoulder, saying:

"So sorry; but I promised my cousin!"

"That fellow, Ravanel, does everything well!" Rob puffed, as he dodged unskillful dancers. "By jingo, cousin, you and he moved as if you were made for each other!"

The girl's feet were suddenly still; her slim hand slid into the boy's arm, and she said rather wearily:

"It is so warm! Let us go on the piazza a moment."

The violins still scraped merrily to twang of the guitars, a half hour later; but mortal feet are not really winged, even in youth, and at last Wythe Dandridge wearied in the flesh—whatever she might have done in spirit—of her new found partner. Eager and flushed, she was listening naively to the pleasant sound of his low-voiced narration, as they strolled through the supper room, past the wide doors of the conservatory and down the narrow walk between the tubs. The place seemed deserted; their slow-moving feet making no sound upon the plank. Suddenly, just at its turn, voices fell clear and sharp through the scented air. A woman's was saying, rather wearily:

"Love is ever but a chance. One should be very sure before confessing; doubly so, before proclaiming it! And you are so young."

The Carolinian halted, quickly as at command; his face grave and stern, as his glance swept rapidly his companion's. Its flush had gone; a wondering query rising in its place; but ere he could turn, the man's rapid answer came:

"Young! Love like mine is born old! *You* know it has lived for *years!* You know how deep and true and honest it is! *You* must understand me!—And I tell you, I must have an answer! I must know if *he* is in my way! I tell you I begin to hate—Ravanel!"

Wythe Dandridge's eyes, wide appealing out of her now ashen face, met those of the man beside her. They were glinting with an ugly light; his lips drawn in and his cheek as pale as her own. But he faced quickly for the door, bending his head as he whispered shortly:

"Come! We are *de trop* here!"

And the girl, resting heavily on his arm, followed his stronger will mechanically as a low, mocking laugh and well-known voice followed them:

"Nonsense! You will learn that I am your truest friend! Love is a delusion, Rob. I know, for I am old enough to be your—aunt!"

CHAPTER V.

UNDER THE STRAIN.

Almost two years had passed since Mrs. Courtenay's ball for the —th Cavalry; years of which the weeks made history so fast, that not even the worst sufferers by its making could count its mile-stones in swift rush by them. Seven Pines and Seven Days had told their tales of strategy and blood and constancy. Riddled Fredericksburg now sat widowed, amid her desolated fields. Twice had the "bare-footed boys" crossed the historic river and marched almost greedily to the feast of death awaiting them on Northern soil; twice had they marched back from carnage that, typing the heroism of both sides to it, was yet void of real result.

The meteor campaign of Stonewall Jackson had made the Valley its deathless name in chronicle; but, too, that fateful blow had fallen which struck closest to the heart of the South, and left the name of Chancellorsville a synonym for woe!

The dull echo of the guns at Vicksburg was heard no more; silenced for aye by that capitulation which, close following the retreat from Gettysburg, made the national day a veritable *dies irae* for the South.

And now the Valley of the Shenandoah had

4

been plowed by hostile batteries; furrowed by the flying hoofs of Federal and Confederate in turn, as raid and campaign came thundering down its defiles, only to be hurled back by the stubborn constancy of their defenders.

Winchester, the once glad queen of the lower Valley, had fairly earned her title of the "race track," given her by General Crook; each height and streamlet for miles around her now made classic by daring dash or stubborn combat; her fair fields, one straggling cemetery for the nameless and the noted dead; her very streets blood spattered and her house fronts bullet scarred, from many a rush through them of pursuer and pursued. Yet, with that filial love for the mother town, peculiarly Virginian, the women of Winchester—and only they were left with youngest stripling and the very aged—sat by their desolated hearths and, almost hopeless, still hoped on.

Worse still, if possible, was the plight of those homes in the Valley, more scattered and remote from the sympathy and encouragement of closer contact; for the scythe of the sword had harvested well. Broad fields, late smiling with plenty, stretched away blackened and bare; tall barns, late filled with food for man and beast, swung open doors before their emptiness, where indeed the torch had left them more than charred skeletons. Stock and implements of production

had alike shriveled in the red flame of war; and
many even of the old family servants had followed
the Will-o'-the-wisp, misnamed Freedom, leaving
the women-tenanted homesteads pitiably helpless.

Crag-Nest was scarce exception to this general
rule; albeit the strong character and clear common sense of its mistress—aided by unusual
storage of supplies and by the steadfast fidelity of
old Ezekiel—had so far kept the war-whelped wolf
somewhat farther from the door.

Heedless alike of advice from friends and ur-
gence by relatives, Mrs. Courtenay had remained
amid her lessening household gods; and there with
her now were Val Courtenay and Wythe Dandridge, the old negro and his aged wife completing
the household.   Little change showed in the
matron's face or figure; the strong lines of the
one perhaps a trifle deeper, the outline of
the other no less firm and erect, albeit the plain
black dress showed somewhat the touch of time.
The elder girl, more grave and thoughtful as a
rule, still upbore bravely under the pressure; the
old time flashes of her saucy merriment sheering
through the gloom about them.   But Wythe, in
her childlike simplicity of nature and her more
matured personal charm, showed more plainly results of "time and the hour."

Gay and grave by turns, she gave way not in-
frequently to possession by the "blue devils"; and

more than once Val had found her in floods of bitter tears, which only strongly worded remonstrance had turned away from the straight road to hysterics. Pale and with more distinct lines beneath her appealing eyes, Wythe was a more attractive woman than in her baby-beauty days, when the —th Cavalry had ridden so gaily to the mountain.

But the most changed part of that household was the whilom stately Ezekiel; gorgeous no longer in his brass-buttoned swallow-tail and wealth of immaculate linen, but replacing both by a doubtful hued army shirt; while the carefully brushed but worn folds of the former were stowed away in hiding in "da loff ov da barn," only to be donned on great occasions of advancing raid, or greater ones of rebel yelling pursuit.

Neither of the girls had met their partners of the ball since that eventful night; and one of them had never voluntarily let the name of hers pass her lips. In their own apartment, Wythe had sometimes introduced the theme, only to have it abruptly changed by her cousin with the curt truth that "there were more serious things to think of"; and now her lips also were sealed on the tacitly tabooed subject.

The morning succeeding the dance the girl had risen pale, sick and feverish; later taking to bed with a sharp attack of what the country doctor pronounced "nervous fever; result of heat, over exercise and excitement." Val, nursing her faithfully for weeks, had been glad of excuse for seeing no visitors, save Rob, in his flying calls each day. But the sick girl only grew restless and pettish, when his messages were faithfully delivered; and all her cousin's coaxing had only drawn from her the stereotyped phrase: "There's no answer." Then, one night the colonel rode over in hot haste and bade them all farewell. A threatened raid by Averell into Western Virginia had brought orders to move at dawn; only temporarily the veteran thought. But weeks passed; and then an infantry regiment moved down the Valley, camping on the cavalry's old ground. Then came the active movements of the spring, and the cavalry was kept on the go about the border; so the women saw no more of their kinsmen.

But in all those long months, Wythe Dandridge never breathed to Val one word of her chance eavesdropping. Gentle, affectionate, and yielding as ever to her stronger cousin, she felt that she had been slighted for her by the youth she thought had loved her; and her pride waited vainly for some confidence from the other side, which might give her the whole story of his proposal to Val, which she felt had been too lightly valued and scornfully refused. So, when no such confidence came, the girl shut up the memory in her sore little heart;

drifting further away on a dreary sea of doubt and vainly striving to give shape to the Elmos-fire of her false imaginings. And Val Courtenay—firmly believing that the pure heart of her one cousin had wandered wholly away from the other, in its reaching for higher conquest of the man she herself had once loved and, as she believed honestly, now despised—waited for some word or hint that would give her ground for serious warning. She had even resolved, in her unselfish watch over her weaker friend, not to spare herself, did it prove needful to tell the whole story of her own trust and of the bitter awakening from it. But word, nor hint, came from the strangely closed lips of the other; and a tacit compact seemed to raise itself between the pair to "let the dead past bury its dead," after its own fashion and in cerements of silence.

At first frequent letters came from Rob Maury to his cousin, filled with query of, and messages to, Wythe. To the former she could give no intelligent reply; for the girl would listen dully to the latter, only repeating her invariable formula: "There's no answer!" So, gradually, the letters grew less frequent; finally ceasing altogether under pressure of distance, active campaigning and other reasons, as Val told herself. For she believed that the boy, like herself, had at least caught the drift of his sweetheart's preference;

and the pride of their common blood sided with and applauded his decision.

Of Rob, however, they still had frequent news in his colonel's letters to Crag-Nest; and these spoke of his good soldiership and refusal of promotion, to stick to his position as chief of the scouts organized by him. The letters also spoke sometimes of Captain Ravanel's good work and upward progress. But from neither direct did any letter now come; Wythe having promptly returned two bulky missives Rob first sent, and that young gentleman having refrained from repetition. But when the colonel's letters came, Mrs. Courtenay would read them aloud and—naturally warming to their theme, amid her present surroundings— would descant volubly upon the grandeur of her kinsman and the noble conduct of his brave boys.

Not wholly cheery were those long evenings around the lamp, in the now barer parlor of Crag-Nest, as the three women plied busy needles on the coarse fabrics for soldiers' needs, with tongues no less busy, when their theme was the suffering and trials of those for whom they wrought. But less cheery still, to the two girls, were those evenings when the colonel's letters came; for then the matron, her needle laid aside, would read aloud, re-read, and descant on them; her hearers sitting with heads bowed over their work and needles flying swifter through it, but with wholly silent tongues.

So the weeks of the summer of '63 dragged their slow lengths along, strangely unbroken to those patient-waiting women, save by rumor of distant strife, and by occasional sounds of distant cannonading, dully echoing from further down the Valley. But one bright, crisp morning Ziek appeared before his mistress, garbed as of yore, save for the frayed edges of his huge standing collar; his great eyes rolling with excitement as he cried:

"Da's comin', Mis' 'Ginia, an' I tinks I better mount Selim an' reckonloiter 'em up da road."

Permission given—for it was the faithful black's habit thus to scout, before each advance of friend or foe—Ezekiel was soon galloping up the Winchester pike, upon the lank mule, now sole component of the Crag-Nest stud. For the slick, horses had long since been impressed for artillery need; and Val—not without secret and bitter tears shed upon his neck, embraced by her fair arms—had long since sent her gallant chestnut to Rob, with a brief line to urge him to use the horse as a man should in his country's need.

CHAPTER VI.

VARYING VISITATIONS.

Once more the lady of Crag-Nest and her two girls waited expectant on the old porch, gazing across the neglected lawn, to the now broken fence and half dismantled gate. About the porch, and the steps leading to it, stood tubs and pots, lifted from the now unsashed conservatory; but some nameless sympathy showed between the plants and their changed mistresses, for they seemed weaker, less thriving and somewhat uncared for in the garish, summer sunlight.

And as the expectant women waited the return of their faithful old courier, the sound of many hoofs advancing rapidly broke upon the air, drawing nearer and nearer, until whirling dust clouds showed about the turn of the hill beyond, and through them emerged the head of a cavalry column. With clatter of hoof and clank of accoutrements, the column—a considerable body—came on and passed the gate; three riders drawing out from its head and turning in toward the house.

"Welcome, my kinsman!" Mrs. Courtenay cried, running down the steps with outstretched hand and glowing face, as she recognized Col. Calvert.

A moment later, the veteran threw himself

from his horse with the agility of a younger man; but still stood erect by his bridle until his companion dismounted more slowly, when both threw their reins to the orderly.

"Ah! Cousin Virginia! As ready of welcome as ever," the colonel cried. "But you know the general, of course. You too, my fair kinswomen," he added to the advancing girls, as he bent his tall head over the old lady's hand; then turning to sweep both fair foreheads with his grim mustache.

"Yes, indeed!" his companion cried with a merry laugh, as he too took the matron's hand. "He were a sorry Virginia trooper that did not know Crag-Nest and its mistress!"

"She were a sorry Virginian, General," the old lady answered with stately courtesy, "who did not feel it honor to welcome one of your name and race under her poor roof. Will you come in and rest a while before luncheon?" she added with a telegraphic glance of warning to Val.

"Thank you, we really have no time. We are on a forced march," the general answered promptly. "But zounds! Colonel, I do envy you the perquisites of that gray mustache! Would I could change it, young ladies, for this foxy one of mine—with the conditions!" And the general's jovial laugh rang out clear, as he stroked his huge brown beard with one hand and hitched up his sword belt around his ample waist with the other.

Rotund and short-necked, but with huge depth of chest and vigorous frame, the noted cavalry chief still looked every inch a soldier. Port and feature alike showed habit of command; and the jovial kindliness of the face spoke out from firm and resolute feature and clear, keen gray eyes. The mouth was hidden by the long reddish mustache that met the heavy beard sweeping half over his chest; and his raised hat showed ruddy masses of hair of similar hue. His dress was the simple shell jacket and high boots; the only rank-marks the three stars and wreath upon his collar and the flowing black plume, caught with a star.

"You have heard the news, Cousin Virginia," the colonel said as his companion's laugh died out. "You know that we have been beaten back from the very edge of a complete success?"

"We have heard it all," the matron said quietly; "Gettysburg, Vicksburg—all! God's ways are the best, Cousin Wirt; but it is very bitter."

"It is all in the fortunes of war, kinswoman," the old man answered. "I am not so sure that Voltaire was wrong; and those fellows at Gettysburg certainly had the heaviest battalions. But I asked the general to stop with me a moment and advise you to take shelter in Richmond."

"Yes; he is right," the general cried bluntly; "Crag-Nest is very exposed and on the direct highway. We do not know surely, but I think, for a while, gray jackets will be scarce in the Valley."

"Are you not to camp near us again?" Wythe asked eagerly.

"No; we are force marching to mass with Hampton," the general answered, with a meaning look at the colonel. "We were the rear guard crossing the river. We both think it safer for you ladies to seek shelter within the lines."

"And wherefore? We have so far been able to protect ourselves from Yankee intrusion—of a personal nature. Even those who took our stock and supplies respected our sex."

"Perhaps, my kinswoman," the colonel replied with a shrug of his broad shoulders; "but then they knew we were always close behind them. From this out we may be——"

"Close in front, with them behind us," the general broke in with a laugh. "But seriously, my dear madam, your kinsman and I stopped solely to give you this warning. Better heed it, while you can."

"This is my home; the only one I have known since girlhood," the old lady said gently, but very firmly. "It is the second home of these dear children; and broken as it is—denuded of so much that could make our friends happy beneath its roof —we love it as we could no other."

"We will be happier here with her, Cousin Wirt; happier here with her than elsewhere," Val Courtenay said advancing to her aunt's side— "and as safe, under His care."

Colonel Calvert only pulled his mustache, perplexed; but the general said bluntly:

"Happier, perhaps, Miss Courtenay, but I doubt the safety. This is not a question of Providence, but of war's necessity. With the Valley overrun and your friends out of reach, you would be cut off and helpless. I strongly advise your removal within our lines, as soon as convenient."

"You had best think seriously of this, Cousin Virginia," the colonel said gravely, "before it is too late."

"I will think of it; and I thank you both for your thought of us;" the old lady answered, her head still erect. "But can not I induce you to stay even for a glass of wine?"

"Impossible, madam. Colonel, we will have to ride hard now to overtake the column," the general answered; and with cordial adieux to the ladies the soldiers were soon in saddle and galloping after the distant dust cloud. The three women stood still and silent until they disappeared; then Mrs. Courtenay cried:

"Why, girls! what want of thought! None of us asked for Rob or Captain Ravanel."

A vivid blush was Wythe's only answer; but

Val Courtenay, placing her slim hand on the blue-veined one, said quietly:

"And shall we move away, aunt?"

"I have promised them," the old lady answered quietly, "I will think about it. But come, my children, while Crag-Nest is our home, we have duties in it." And the three Virginian women turned their backs upon the bright sunshine and moved into the silent house. All that day and the next Ezekiel did not reappear; and the lonely women wondered at his absence. But they did not grow uneasy, for there was no hint of enemy in the Valley; and they merely supposed that, taking the wrong road, he had missed the friendly column, and had wearied out his old mule in search for it. But in the diminished household his absence was seriously felt, though the girls cheerfully did all they could to fill his place and lessen the extra burthens upon the old negress. But on the second evening, speculation ran into uneasiness; and the girls tramped several miles to the nearest neighbor to make inquiries and organize a search. It was quite dark when they returned without news; and doubt and fatigue made the simple supper quieter and more gloomy than ever before. That nameless foreboding which oppresses sometimes without cause, seemed to weigh upon the household, sealing their lips like lead; and the women separated early. Kissing her aunt for

good-night, Val Courtenay paused an instant; then
said gravely:

"I have been thinking over their warning, aunt.
As we walked across the mountain it seemed more
lonely and desolate than ever before. Perhaps it would be safer to leave home—for the
present."

"In the hands of Providence, my child, we are
as safe in one place as another," the old lady answered calmly. "Surely you do not fear these insolent invaders more than before. They have
visited us often enough to be too familiar to dread.
But, never mind. As I promised my kinsman; I
will think about it!"

In their own room, the girls were soon ready
for rest; and Wythe quickly yielded to fatigue and
slept deeply, if restlessly. Val placed her tallow
dip in its tall, silver candlestick upon the night
stand, her watch near it, and was about to follow
her cousin, when the latter tossed in her sleep and
spoke broken words:

"Come back to me—miss you so—know I need
you now—never loved Val—," were the disjointed
phrases that fell upon her ear. Pale as her soft
gown, the girl bent upon the sleeper glowing eyes,
and a smile in which pity struggled with contempt curled her lips.

"Poor little fool!" she said slowly to herself.
"Can she really love that—pshaw! It must be a

passing fancy only; but he—the double traitor, to dare! And under this roof—before my very face! —Oh! she can not, really—but poor old Rob? To throw him over so, without one word!"—She paused as the other spoke again—"That man's name! Silly child, you scarce deserve my pity. That, and my contempt I should keep for myself!"

Moving noiselessly, she passed to the old-time bureau, candle in hand; softly opened a drawer and took up a tiny casket. Then she stood staring at it a while; swift emotions chasing each other across her face as her eyes riveted upon the lid. Raising them suddenly, the woman caught her reflection in the mirror, tall, weird and ghost-like in the fitful candlelight; and vivid blush dyed the oval of her face and slim, soft curves of neck, at her own expression. Then the color died away, the face hardened into resolution and the lips set firm and almost cruel, as she sprung the casket's lid with firm hand. From it she took a yellow, time-stained note; a dance-card and a dry and crumbling rosebud—white once but now black, powdering as she moved it with quick gesture of disgust:

"Better one fool than two," she whispered through set teeth. "Why should I keep these milestones on my fool's errand of the past? What is it to me who cares for him now! Fraser Rava-

nel, God knows I do not hate you! May He forgive
me for despising you!"

One quick clinch of the slim, nervous hand, and
the dry bud was powder in it. Then slowly, but
not trembling, that hand held the little note and
dance-card in the sickly flame; the set lips once
more curling into contemptuous curves, as the
paper crinkled and blackened, then fell into a
little heap of gray ash.

Slowly the girl turned; once more set the
candle upon the stand, and placed the solid silver
extinguisher over the soft tallow. Then she sunk
noiselessly upon her knees, rested her forehead
upon the coverlid and prayed long and silently.
At last she rose, calm and placid; laid her head
upon the pillow and slept at once.

How long had passed she knew not; but suddenly Val Courtenay found herself sitting bolt upright; wide awake and listening intently. Even
through the closed windows, the tramp of horses
came plainly to her ear; and they were rapidly
approaching the house. Springing up she threw
a wrapper about her, and passed to the window,
peering into the hazy gloom without. Then, her
eyes growing more accustomed to the dusky light,
she saw dim forms of horsemen moving swiftly up
the path; some halting directly in front of the
house, while others deployed right and left to sur-
round it. Plainly they were Federals, for she

5

knew that friends would take no such precaution; but, ere she had time to move, a familiar voice broke quavering upon the night:

"Mis' 'Ginia! Missus! The gennelmuns axes ter be recebed."

Passing swiftly to the bedside. Val touched her sleeping cousin lightly, saying, as she lit her candle:

"Don't be frightened, dear. The Yankees are here. Dress quickly and come down. *I* am going to aunt."

She lit the second candle as she spoke and passed from the room, the fitful gleam of the light she held aloft projecting fantastic shadows across the broad hall, that, in the midnight stillness, had frightened many a woman, in other days than this. But recking nothing of them, the girl passed rapidly down the broad stair only to find the hall door already open and the tall, erect, black figure of her aunt, silhouetted against the gleam of the candle sputtering in the night wind. And as she hastened downward, Val caught the clear voice— no more perturbed than if ordering a glass refilled at her own table:

"Ezekiel, why are you disturbing us at this unseemly hour? Dismount at once and go to your own room."

"Dismount, sir!" echoed a clear voice from the darkness without. There was a sound of quickly given orders; a clank of sabers in dismounting and the click of four carbines brought to a ready. Next instant heavy boots tramped up the broad steps and the tall officer in blue, flanked by Ezekiel on the left, stood facing the lady, within the taper's feeble gleam; while just around it dimly showed the muzzles of the carbines; and at the moment Val Courtenay passed to her aunt's side, without a word, but placing her hand quietly upon her arm in token of support.

"What has come over you, Ezekiel?" Mrs. Courtenay queried, calmly ignoring the enemy's presence. "I send you on an errand, you stay unseemly time and return with strange men at midnight."

"'For' da Lor! Mis' 'Ginia, I dunna mysef," Ezekiel began, forgetting all his dignity in the emergency. "Da Yankee gennelmuns jess nabbed da ole man——"

"It is not his fault, madam. Permit me to explain," the tall soldier broke in, not discourteously. "We were hanging on Fitz Lee's flank; but his rear guard, under that old firebrand Calvert, held us off——"

"Pardon me, sir," Mrs. Courtenay interrupted with perfect calmness. "As a perfect stranger, I may save you awkwardness by stating that the gentleman you refer to is my kinsman."

"You have reason to be proud of him, madam,"

the officer replied, passing his gauntlet over his
mustache to repress a smile. "Briefly, your people outnumbered and outrode us; we were forced
to by-paths, picked up this sable gentleman, and
found him as well known to the country side as
your home is to us, madam. His detention is our
fault. We have information that old—ahem!—
Colonel Calvert, and perhaps bigger game, are under your roof. The house is surrounded, escape is
impossible. We want them." So speaking the
officer advanced one step toward the door; the old
negro making quick side step toward his mistress
and promptly facing him.

"Stand aside, Ezekiel," Mrs. Courtenay said
quietly, "I can not see our late visitors. To you,
sir, I can only say that you are much too late. The
only occupants of this house are three ladies—all
unarmed. I regret extremely that you did not
arrive while my kinsman and his friends *were* here;
for they had given you more fitting reception for a
soldier."

"I am extremely sorry, madam, to discommode
you," the officer answered quietly. "I am Major
Buford, of the — Pennsylvania Cavalry. I am in-
formed that these rebel officers are here; and even
at the risk of incurring your displeasure, it is my
duty to convince myself that I am wrong."

"And pray, sir, if my word be insufficient,
how do you propose to do this?" The old

lady's voice trembled slightly, but plainly not from fear.

"I regret that I shall be compelled to search the house, madam," the officer answered decisively. "I shall give you as little discomfort as possible. Already my men are doing as much for the outbuildings. Pardon me, it will not take long."

As he spoke he pointed with his sword to lanterns flashing here and there about the open barn and deserted negro quarters, and again raising his hat he moved one step toward the door.

The lady of the house stepped back from the entrance, her right hand holding the candle steadily aloft, while her left gently sought her niece's, as though to restrain her.

"We are defenseless women," she said, with much the air "The Austrian" might have used to the rabble in the palace; "the sole resistance we can make is protest. If, sir, your duty forces you to violate the proprieties of my home, I myself will conduct you. Come, sir; this is our drawing room." She flared the candlelight into the empty room, as the soldier crossed the portal and doffed his hat. "Valerie, my child, I must not leave you alone; come with us."

"Pardon me, madam," the Federal said, glancing into every corner of the bare room, "but permit the negro to pilot us. The gentlemen we look for are not apt to come for the asking. Our inter-view might prove unpleasant, if nothing more, to you ladies."

"In my husband's day," the matron answered gravely, "he permitted no stranger to enter these rooms unescorted. As his representative, I must show you no less consideration. Come, sir. Time must be precious to you, and we are wasting it." She crossed the hall as she spoke, throwing wide the door of her well-loved dining room; the Federal at her right side, pistol in hand, and four dis-mounted troopers with ready carbines bringing up the rear.

So the strange procession passed the lower rooms and clanked up the broad stairway; silent and weird as the phantom host that leaguered the walls of Prague. One after another the doors of the vacant rooms were thrown wide by the firm hand of their mistress, only to be proved bare and tenantless to closest scrutiny. But reaching the door facing the stair's head, Val stepped swiftly forward and stretched her arm across the casing. The officer, with quick gleam in his eye, made movement to advance; but the girl, catching his ex-pression, even in the dim light, answered it as quietly as clearly:

"You mistake, sir. I only mean that this is a lady's room." She rapped quickly on the door, raising her voice as she finished:

"Wythe, are you dressed?" For answer the door·swung wide, and even the rough troopers stared at the pretty vision of the fair girl within; pale and wide-eyed, with golden hair rippling loose to the knees of her dark gown. Timorously, but with brave effort to be calm, Wythe stepped forward and joined her kinswomen. But she carried in her hand the tall silver candlestick, leaving the room behind her in darkness.

A quick smile twitched the mustache of the Federal soldier, but his eye never left the windows reflecting the candlelight through the gloom, as he said:

"Your pardon, Mrs. Courtenay, but we must search this room. The delay makes it possible that our quarry is here."

For the first time the old lady's lips trembled, and the angry flash came to her eye, as the full, rounded chin raised higher, and she began:

"Sir! I have said that this apartment is—"

"Ours, aunt!" Val broke in quietly. "Wythe and I will open our bureau drawers and hat boxes, if these—" she paused before the word— "gentlemen will stand here and cover us with their carbines!"

Suiting action to word, she made a quick sign to the other girl; the two passed into the room, placing their candles on the bureau and rapidly opening the deep, old-fashioned closets and throw-

ing dresses and wraps hanging in them, out upon
the floor.   Turning to the heavy, carved bedstead
they wheeled it away from the wall; and then the
elder girl turned to the quiet soldier at the door
and asked:

"You are satisfied, I hope, sir?"

The officer again passed his gauntlet swiftly
across his mustache; but he answered gravely and
courteously:

"May I enter one instant?"   And not waiting
for permission he strode across to the window and,
raising the sash, peered below.   Noting the sheer
drop, without cornice or foothold without, he
turned again to the hall; asked, by sign only, for
one of the candles and, raising it high above his
head, scanned the solid ceiling for trap-door, or
roof-scuttle.   Seeing sign of none, he turned to the
matron and said quietly:

"You must comprehend, madam, how unpleasant it is for us to have disturbed your rest and
made ourselves your unbidden guests.   Duty,
though not always pleasant, must be performed.
And now, ladies, I will relieve you of our presence;
satisfied that our men are not here, at least in the
house."

"They are not here at all, sir," Mrs. Courtenay
replied haughtily.   "Had they been, no daughter
of the Cabbells had misstated the fact.   But I
must repeat my regret that they are miles away,

with their commands; else your reception had been more fitting than an old woman and two girls could possibly offer. As your duty here is finished, I bid you good-night, sir! Ezekiel, attend these gentlemen."

His bow received by slightest inclination of her stately head, the speaker moved to the stair head, standing aside to let him pass; the black gravely led the way down the dusky passage and the troopers clanked down behind their leader. A moment later the recall sounded without; the scattered squads assembled for report of failure; and then the party trotted briskly down the path and were heard clattering along the hard pike beyond.

"Oh! Aunt, how trying it must have been to you!" Val cried, caressing the still grim old lady. "But you must have known I would come; why did you go to the door alone?"

"It is my place to receive all visitors to Crag-Nest, my child, be they friends or foes. But—" her rare smile came to the firm lips—"you are brave children, and do not shame your blood. There are some hours to dawn; go to bed and sleep away recollection of this—intrusion!"

She kissed both girls gently; but Wythe cried suddenly:

"Oh! Aunt Virginia, they were right! We had better seek shelter in the lines."

"Go to sleep, my children," was the quiet answer. "I promised our kinsman that I would think about it." She passed slowly down the stair; her voice coming back to them in the quiet order: "Lock the front door, Ezekiel, and go to bed!"

CHAPTER VII.

THE FIRST QUARREL.

Once more summer was smiling serenely upon the Valley, ripening her sorely needed crops— however Nature may have had cause to frown upon man's brutalizing her fair domain with hoof and steel and torch. For in the months between, the old familiar battle-ground had had little rest; and, while great armies watched each other elsewhere, as bloodhounds in the leash, raid and incursion from either side still scarred the bosom of the "Daughter of the Stars."

Grant was now thundering at the Petersburg-back-door of the coveted capital of rebeldom; but, as diversion, Jubal Early had twice hurled Jackson's old soldiers across the Potomac—once threatening Washington herself—then, in stern reprisal, laying Chambersburg in ashes. But the wisdom of Lee now calls him back to guard that teeming granary, so vital to the needs of both their armies; for the Valley must be held at any cost, at least until those precious crops are garnered, and stored beyond the reach of raid.

And now Sheridan—massing all force available in the lower Valley—fronts Early; cognizant as himself of vast results to come from his protec-

tion of it, or from the Federals forcing him beyond
this fecund base of bread for country and for army
alike.

It is now mid-August, 1864, and the ladies of
Crag-Nest still sit in its barer halls, now overlooking wholly waste fields and ruined outbuildings.
For, during all those intervening months, Mrs.
Courtenay had been "thinking about it," but had
never brought herself to leave that well loved roof.
Indeed, she rejoiced many a time that home love
had triumphed over discretion; for often the home
—converted for the nonce into a hospital—added
to the comfort, if, indeed, it had not saved the lives,
of sorely wounded friends; sometimes of maimed
and suffering foes.

For the grand hospitality that gave Crag-Nest
its fame of yore was drawn from that highest
source which teaches that the thirsting enemy be
given drink; and more than one blue coated raider
had limped back to camp, blessing the tender touch
of womanhood in that Valley home, and had sent
its fame to gladden anxious hearts about distant
fire-sides. But now the plants and shrubs—still
more neglected and dejected looking than before—
remained always out of doors; rough bunks and
cots, spread with clean but coarse sheeting, changing their late resting place to a real conservatory
for the sick.

Tenantless now, the prim white row of narrow

beds still spoke readiness for the worst; while the old lady and Val Courtenay paced the now dingy piazza, with slow step and quiet talk.

"It will be a true pleasure, my child," the old lady was saying, as she unfolded her well creased letter and read with unaided eyes, "to have our kinsman as guest once more. See, he writes that he commands a brigade under Early; and that he will be in easy distance of the home."

"We may expect him by morning," the girl answered absently; her eyes fixed upon the tall, blue mountain top she and another had once watched from the window, with the moon upon it.

"Yes, in the morning, my dear; and Wythe is now putting the finishing touches to their room. Major Ravanel and Lieutenant Robert Maury, his adjutant, will be with our cousin. It will seem like old times, my child, to have the three under our roof once more."

"Dear old Rob," Val answered earnestly, "he must have proved quite a hero, to have promotion forced on him against his will."

"He is of our blood, my dear, and naturally did his duty," her aunt answered calmly, "and Major Ravanel, too! Well, 'good blood can not lie.' I wonder if he is as *distingue* as formerly."

"Doubtless," Val answered, forcing herself to the brief reply.

"Of course, my dear." The old lady folded the

letter, placing it in the bosom of her worn black gown. "It is his right of birth. The Ravanels are an old family, wealthy; and the major is an only child."

The girl's eyes came back from the mountain top, but looked straight ahead, as she answered coldly:

"Yes, aunt; his ma doubtless is very proud of Major Ravanel."

Something in the tone made the old lady cast a quick, searching glance upon the speaker; but delicate courtesy of the old school refrained from comment, as the girl turned into the house with the words:

"Poor little Wythe! I must go and look after her."

She passed up the broad stair, the fading light falling across a face calm but resolved; and, entering the open room where her cousin, flushed with exercise, was viewing her completed work, she said quietly:

"Wythe, dear, have you finished?" But, her own glance answering her question, she took the other girl's hand gravely and led her to the window; both seating themselves in the low seat made by its broad sill, as she added:

"It is a long time since these old rooms have been used."

"Not since the —th Cavalry first came to the

Valley," the younger girl replied quickly. "Oh! Val, how long ago that does seem!"

Miss Courtenay's face was turned toward the far crests of the Massanutten. For a moment she made no reply, speaking then with her eyes still studying the mountain top.

"Wythe, I have never alluded to that time," she said gently; "but I have thought much of it since."

There was no answer, in words; but an eloquent one might have been translated from the other's sudden flush and decided pout, had her cousin's eyes been upon her. So, innocent of random shot that told, the former went on:

"We will meet them again to-morrow morning. I hope, Wythe, you will be considerate of Rob's feelings."

"Are they so very delicate that they need nursing?" Miss Dandridge queried sharply. "If so, Aunt Virginia might prepare a cot in the hospital for him!"

The unusual tone and manner turned Val's eyes from the crest to the speaker.

"I am surprised!" she said quietly. "You sneer at Rob Maury as though he were a stranger and an enemy, rather than the friend of your girlhood!"

"A woman's tastes may change, I suppose," was the answer, given with a pert toss of the fair

head. "I have always been polite and just to—
your cousin, I hope. He certainly has no right
to expect anything more."

"I am not sure of that, Wythe. He had at
least the right to expect cordiality of old friend-
ship; and, that failing him, to be told the reason—"

"Young soldiers can usually supply their own
reasons for their acts," the girl cried, her cheeks
ablaze and her tiny slipper tapping angrily on the
floor.

"Proper pride—justice to you, might have prevented his supposing that a passing fancy—"

"Passing fancy!—Well!—I think we had better not discuss this further, Valerie Courtenay! I
don't know that I need any advice; and I'm very
sure that I have asked none!" And Miss Dandridge rose from the window sill and stood angrily
facing her cousin; her graceful head thrown back
and her blue eyes lit with an angry light, that Val
had never seen in them before.

"No, Wythe," she answered quietly; "for the
first time in our lives, my little sister has shut her
heart to me. You know I have never intruded on
it; have never violated delicacy before. But, dear,
these are sad, dangerous days. Men are cut off
suddenly from those they love; and you would
never cease repenting injustice to a brave, true
gentleman—"

"He's a perfect boy!" Wythe exclaimed with much heat. "Pshaw! he doesn't have a feeling deeper than *that!*" and her rosy little thumb marked a half inch against the elevated little finger. "As for justice, well, I should think he—Val! We *have* been friends, almost sisters, *so* long. You are older than I, but there are some cases where it is best that advice should not be given until it is asked—No; don't misunderstand. I have never blamed *you*, dear."

"Blamed me?" the older girl's eyes widened in amaze.

"No! *You* could not help it! *You* could not prevent a man's fancy changing from one woman to another; and the chance that threw Major Ravanel with me—"

"Wythe! What *do* you mean? What right have you to dream such a thing!"

This time it was Val's face that flushed hotly; its lines hardened and lips set firm, as the full bust rose and fell.

"Dreams sometimes come true," the other girl answered, tossing her head. "People should be careful what they say, and where they say it, if others are to be catechised. Major Ravanel and I—"

She broke off abruptly before the quick, commandful gesture. The other woman stood erect now; her tall head towering above her friend and

6

her voice cold and slow under coercion of her strong will, as she said:

"Enough of this! I see now that I was wise to refrain before; very foolish to have ventured now one word of warning."

"I needed no warning, thank you." Wythe spoke rapidly but defiantly; no yielding in her tone, or pose, before the strong anger and reproach of the other, as she added:

"The girl who needs one once, is—unfortunate; the second time, she is—a fool!"

Val Courtenay's face was eloquent, if her lips remained silent. Twice they moved, as though about to answer; but the well trained will reasserted itself, and without a word she moved slowly from the room and down the broad stairs.

Left to herself, Wythe stood erect and defiant; a plump, blonde Pythoness for the instant. Then the hot, flushed face changed; the red lips filling to a decided pout, while a sort of wonder crept into the wide blue eyes.

"I don't care," she cried aloud to herself. "It's too bad! Val and I never quarreled before; but it's all *his* fault! The idea to be thrown over like that, and then have *her* lecture me about my injustice to him! I hope I was not mean to Val. It *is* his fault if I *was*, and—I don't—I believe I don't care one bit!" And to prove it, the spoiled child here dominated the newly asserted

woman, and Wythe Dandridge—throwing herself
face downward on the colonel's freshly smoothed
bed—indulged in the solace of a good old-time
cry.

But the tears of pure-hearted girlhood are but
April showers; and soon the sobs ceased and the
girl jumped up, with the rather irrelevant exclamation:

"Lor! It's quite sundown; and what must my
eyes look like!"

But hasty application of cool spring water soon
made the pretty, blue optics themselves again;
and, after hastily smoothing the colonel's rumpled
coverlid, and taking a satisfactory look at her reflected self in the old mirror, Wythe ran down the
steps as though there were no such thing as war,
foreign or domestic. She found Val, too, her self-
contained and placid self; and the frugal supper
passed as usual, with no restraint between the
girls from their first passage at arms. And that
night—when the matron kissed both and begged
them retire early to welcome their guests betimes
—Wythe slipped her hand into her cousin's very
gently; and the differing, yet loving, pair ascended
to their room without a word. Silently they prepared for rest; but when the rosy, pleading face
of the younger—rosebud-fresh as it peered above
the snowy frill of her gown—came close to Val's
pale, thoughtful one, her long, graceful arms went

out and took it to her bosom with the tender love of motherhood; and her lips, now quivering, pressed close upon the soft, fair hair before she said:

"You were right, and I wrong, little sister! There are some things which we must leave to heaven, and our own thoughts and hearts only. But, Wythe, dear, we have had our first angry word—and our last. I do not ask you to forgive me, for I know you have already."

"Forgive! Why you dear old Val—;" the fair face was close against the dark one now and the rosebud lips pressed the firm ones close and long— "you have been everything to me; and I would not have one reproachful look from you for the love of every man in the army of the Valley!"

CHAPTER VIII.

A PORTRAIT EXCHANGED.

Next morning's sun was still young when Colonel Calvert rode up the now grass-grown avenue from the broken gate; Ravanel and Rob Maury following, and a courier behind them, and reined up before the broad but rather rickety steps of the well-remembered piazza.

But early as it was, the lady of the manor again stood there with outstretched hand and gentle smile to welcome them.

"Ah! Cousin Virginia! As ever, upon the advanced picket of hospitality," the veteran cried, as he dismounted from his tall war-horse and strode gaily up the steps; his long saber clanking at his heels. And he bent his mustache to the white, blue-veined hand extended graciously, as he added:

"But where are your fair young aides?"

"They are hastening your breakfast, Cousin Wirt," the lady replied, as though a feudal suzeraine welcoming her liege lord. "Yet I fear it will not prove all that we might wish for such welcome guests."

"And I have brought them two most unwilling captives," he answered with a laugh, as he turned to his courier and added in lower tone as the horses were led away:

"The larger bag on your saddle, Conyers, is to be given the old negro man at once."

"I am sure my cousin slanders you, young gentlemen," Mrs. Courtenay said to the others, as she gave them her hands. "Else our poor reception of the past must linger with you still."

"The colonel knows we are only too glad to come, always," Rob Maury answered awkwardly, and with reddening face. "I only said that it was my duty to stay with the brigade, because I'm so green and am to act as its adjutant-general now."

"And I could never have suggested riding by your gate, Mrs. Courtenay," the young major added in his soft, quiet way, "had there not been some urgent need for corrected maps of the by-roads above—"

"Which can easily be made from here, if I may occupy Crag-Nest with an armed force for one day," the colonel finished for him, as he rejoined them on the piazza. "You see I assume command of my brigade to-morrow; and this brevet captain"— he laid his hand kindly upon Rob's shoulder—"also has general orders to write, details to make and all his plans to lay to catch Sheridan. But here is our little Lily of the Valley!"

Verily Wythe looked the title, as she came into the framing of the great door, more timidly than

her wont; her eyes cast down and her cheeks showing pale even against the ruffle of her pure white
morning-dress. Straight from the kitchen—where
heat and rapid aid to Val and the old negress
might well have flushed her—the girl's face remained quiet and pale as she greeted the colonel
and felt his lips upon her brow, but it colored to
the root of her fair hair, as the Carolinian quickly
advanced and cordially extended his hand.

"I am *so* glad to see you again, Major Ravanel,"
she said rapidly, "even if your title is changed."

"Many things have changed since we last met,
Miss Dandridge," he answered quietly, "and not
all of them for the better—though you are one of
the exceptions."

"And I hope I am not unwelcome," Rob blurted
out, with lamentable want of tact for a brigade
officer. "You see, busy as we were, the colonel insisted we should stop and— " He ceased abruptly,
blushing like a girl, as the awkwardness of his
own speech struck him.

"Aunt Virginia would never have forgiven
him, had he not," Wythe answered calmly, but not
looking at him. And somehow she chanced to
drop her handkerchief; and—stooping for it at the
same moment as the major—failed to see his half
extended hand, as she finished:

"And here is Val. *She* will be so glad, too!"

"Indeed I am!" that young woman answered

for herself, coming out into the morning light, with
a deepened tint upon her cheek, for which the
kitchen fire might have been excuse. "Cousin
Wirt, I began to fear you were indeed a deserter.
And you, dear old Rob! and with shoulder straps
at last!" She turned from the veteran's salute,
extending both hands to the boy; not moving her
handsome head, as she added: "And I congratu-
late you, too, Major Ravanel, upon your promotion."

"Which makes it all the more valuable, Miss
Courtenay," he answered, as he unclasped his
sword belt.

"Oh! let me take it for you, and hang it on the
rack!" Wythe cried, her blue eyes widening at
Val's warmth to one man and coolness to the other.
Her plump little hands captured the shining steel
scabbard; but his retained the belt, as the mock
contention carried them within the hall, toward
the many-antlered head that served for rack, just
within it. And the eyes of each cousin without
saw those of the other follow the maneuver;
though the lips of neither noted it.

"But this is no more gracious welcome," the
old lady exclaimed, "than we gave Major Buford,
of Pennsylvania, when he came hunting you and
the general, Cousin Wirt."

"We had a great laugh over that letter, Cousin
Virginia," Rob cried, "though we were too sorry

the Yank did not find us really here. The colonel read us your account, down at Petersburg. Why you and Cousin Val acted like a pair of heroes."

"There was little heroism about it," the old lady answered quietly. "And Wythe, too, behaved beautifully, for a girl!"

And that young lady hanging the saber on the antlers, blushed as she heard the praiseful words; tinting deeper as her companion added:

"I am sure you always would, Miss Dandridge. But you have not let your household forget me, I hope, because I am unfortunate enough not to be a Virginian."

"Indeed, I have not," she answered frankly. "We have constantly spoken of you, quite as one of us; even when we had no letters from Cousin Wirt."

"I am sure you have," the man went on earnestly. "*You* are the sort of woman any man may trust. I have never forgotten your promise, that night at the ball."

And Val Courtenay, following the older couple through the doorway, caught the last words; and across her now pale face swept the same expression of mingled pity and contempt that had marked it, in the upper room, the previous afternoon.

Complex indeed are the hidden springs that move that machine of mysteries, a woman's heart;

for—had her own life hung in the balance of her
truth-telling—neither one of that gentle pair could
have put into words the feelings in her bosom, as
Wythe caught the look that told she was over-
heard. Blushing deeply, but with head defiantly
erect, she spoke some commonplace to the handsome soldier beside her; but her own voice sounded
as meaningless to her as did the half-unheard reply
in the man's soft tone.

Just then, Ezekiel—with more collar than
usual rearing above the much-brushed blue coat—
announced:

"Da mistus's breckfus am served!"

The three couples moved into the bough-decked
dining room; and—appetite replacing analysis in
the young adjutant's mental outfit—the guests
were soon busy with the viands pressed upon them
by their gentle hostess. But it was a meal far
different from that last one—so clearly remembered by them all—which the military trio had
eaten under that roof; far more different still from
what that matron's will had spread before her
guests, had Crag-Nest's larder compared, in any
sort, with the hospitable ambition of its mistress.
And yet, simple and meagre as that breakfast
really was, the men so plainly enjoying it had lost
all zest had they known they were assisting at the
sad rites over the last lone rooster on the place;
that the light corn-waffles and the yellow eggbread

represented an unusual gap in the well-guarded meal-can; and that their praise of old Esther-- helpmate to Ezekiel—should justly have fallen to the fair hands and pleasure-glowing cheeks of the young girls, who now sauced the viands of their own construction with pleasant talk that echoed nothing of the late awkwardness without.

"Ezekiel, the colonel's plate," Mrs. Courtenay cried gaily, breakfasting herself only on a muffin —"Just one joint of the chicken, Cousin Wirt?"

"Not one scrap, my dear madam!" the veteran beamed, detaining the delicate, old-time china. "Zounds! I have breakfasted like Lucullus, and Esther is a Parisienne in dark masquerade!   I tell you I have often eaten, at the *Trois Freres Proven- ceaux* itself, a specially prepared *bombarde d'cere- risses a la Murat* that had not the delicate flavor of that chicken! The Yankees have left Virginia little else, but they have not captured all her cooks!"

"For your sakes," the old lady answered with a flush of pleasure, "I deeply regret that they have left so little for the cooks' skill.   Especially, Cousin Wirt, I would excuse our 'potato-coffee', knowing your love for the real berry; and that you, sir-- " she bent her head graciously to the Carolinian—"are great coffee drinkers in your own state."

" 'Better a dinner of herbs, where love is'—eh,

my dear?" the veteran cried across the table to
Val; but, unnoting her quick flush, he nodded to
Ezekiel, who moved from the room more swiftly
than his butler's dignity generally permitted.

"Experience teaches that many of our supposed
necessities are merely habits," the young major
said gravely. "In camp, of course, it makes no
difference to us, for parched peas in a tin cup are
nectar, when we have time to make 'coffee.' But
ma writes me that even her delicate taste does not
reject parched wheat, or potato, when no block-
ader has managed to slip into Wilmington for
months."

"I hope your mother has not forgotten me, sir,"
the hostess answered. "Pray write her of the
great pleasure it gives us all to have you under
our roof again. I hope our troubles have not aged
her."

"Not one bit!" Rob Maury cried, pouring black
sorghum over his sixth waffle. "You'd think, from
her photograph, that the major's mother was his
sister. Show Cousin Virginia her picture, major."

The Carolinian's face was very grave; and he
answered no word, as his hand went into the breast
of his shell jacket, drew out a worn photograph
and passed it quickly to his hostess. She took it
with a bow; studying the face long and closely,
ere she said:

"She is wonderfully well preserved, but I think

I would recognize the lips and chin anywhere.
And she has your eyes, sir; and the same black
hair. Ah!" a sigh moved the worn silk on her
bosom as she added gently: "Time has had some
bitterness for us both since we met; but he has
touched her most lightly. See, my dear, this is
my old schoolmate."

As she spoke, she handed the picture to Val;
Rob, at her left hand, leaving his waffle to pass it
to his cousin. But, as his eyes fell upon the face,
he cried bluntly:

"Why, major, this isn't your ma! It's the other
one the mess tried to tease you—"

For once the cool Carolinian's poise was lost.
A burning flush rose to his very forehead, as he
stretched his hand nervously across the table, and
his voice was hard and commandful as he cried:

"Return it, sir! a silly carelessness!"

But even then his eyes flashed into those of the
woman opposite, to find them lifted from the picture to his own, one instant only. But in that
space he read the same contempt they spoke at
the riverside, two long years ago; and they spoke,
too, recognition of a face and figure seen but once
before. Then, self discipline triumphant, he was
himself again; and the voice was soft and gentle
that said to his hostess:

"I beg your pardon for my carelessness, Mrs.
Courtenay; and ma's for mistaking her picture for

any other—" a quick flash of his eyes went out to Val—"*lady's,* value that as I may."

As he spoke, his hand again went to his breast, returning the picture and then proffering another to the old lady, as he added:

"You see ma's hair is as white as your own; that of the other lady has no silver in it."

"I ask your pardon, cousin!" the colonel here cried out, as Ezekiel bore in a massive silver salver, crowned with a venerable tin coffee-pot. But I could not resist a little surprise for you. Mrs. Ravanel sent her boy a rare present of blockade coffee; and he disobeyed orders and forced half of it upon me. Now—smell that! and there's enough in the bag to last my cousins a month!"

The grateful, but long unknown, aroma steamed from the tin, now set before the hostess. But an aroma yet more subtile and far reaching seemed to fill the space between, as the proud old eyes—moist and gentle now—bent upon the veteran; the unseen essence of that love and selflessness, which permeated all who wrought and suffered in those days; without which all had long since yielded to the wearing strain.

The brave, gentle woman—dauntless before all threatened peril—yielded to the more gentle assault upon her. The soft afterglow was on the aged face, and her lips trembled in their effort to form the brief words:

"My kinsman, we thank you!"

Then the delicate tact of both spared further words; the colonel deftly changing the talk to reminiscence of that far past, in Paris; of that so different one, more recent and nearer home.

"Yes; everything is most uncertain," he said at last. "I am not hopeless at all; but we can not close our eyes to the dire need for more men. We have learned to live pretty well without supplies, and to fight fairly without arms. But thinned ranks can not be filled by sheer will; and Grant's boast was fact, that he has forced us to 'rob the cradle and the grave.' Why, Cousin Virginia, Rob there is a veteran to some lads sent me lately; and I am a very youth to some old men at Petersburg— I am sure that General Lee feels this truth; and —though he speaks nothing of it—I feel that he wishes the worst was met and over with. But the president is adamantine; a man with eyes and ears that he can force to see and hear only from within. Both know the dire need of holding this Valley; but Sheridan knows it, too. A great soldier that! And he is facing Early with overwhelming numbers, and can add to them at will; while we— Well!"—he broke off, pulling his huge mustache thoughtfully a moment; then adding courteously: "But, ladies, I ask your forgiveness for talking thus to you. Long exchange from the drawing-room for the camp must plead my excuse. And now, major and Master Rob, look at that!"

As he spoke, he pointed to the huge, upright clock, carved and ponderous, that faced them across the hall; and ere he finished, its strong chime rang out ten times upon the still summer morning.

"As we are, none of us, 'laggards in love,' gentlemen," he added, bowing to his hostess as he rose, "neither must we be in war. This is most pleasant, ladies; but duty is the stern mistress of pleasure in these days. Mr. Maury, we must get to our orders and details. Major Ravanel, you had best mount as soon as possible; and—with your permission, Cousin Virginia—Ziek can serve his country. He will be an invaluable guide for cross-roads and short cuts, major, for some miles about here."

So the breakfast party broke up; and Rob Maury sat, coatless and warm, before great piles of muster rolls and orders, busily at work; the colonel, also coatless, sitting bolt upright in the chair facing him, and aiding by a frequent brief nod, or rarer quick, short word of suggestion.

Half an hour later Wythe Dandridge looked from the window of the kitchen—where the presence of both girls was more necessary, in preparing dinner, from the old negro's service to his country—and saw the engineer officer mount his horse at the barn. The negro was already mounted on the courier's steed; and the officer, having examined his pistol and returned it to the holster, made some hasty notes in a memorandum book, motioned to his companion, and both cantered across the bare field through a gap in the fence and disappeared in the woods beyond.

"He's riding the black, Val," the girl cried. "I wonder what has become of dear little Santee!"

"How should I know?" the other answered quietly. "I think this will do, Aunt Esther. Don't have the fire too fast."

There was silence for a long while; only broken then, and through all that summer day, on technicalities, as the girls went cheerily enough about their household duties; later sitting with their aunt, over rough sewing, until dinner time. By that, the young adjutant was more weary than after a day's march or a hot skirmish; and the meal was quite ready when the major returned, sunburned and dusty, but seemingly content with his day's work. He went straight to the colonel's room for report; the three gentlemen coming down together.

Serious matters seemed to engross them all; for the talk was less cheery than at breakfast, and the colonel declared an early departure necessary, to profit by the young moon. So, sitting together on the broad piazza, until the horses were brought around, there was no chance for *tete-a-tete* among the young people, even had any of the four shown

7

disposition for it. Rob talked apart with his cousin, seriously and low; and Wythe, rather absent mannered, seemed a trifle wearied of the major's quiet speech and coolly courteous manner. The colonel, too, was grave and preoccupied, often reverting to the coming struggle for the possession of the Valley. And finally he said:

"It is more than a year, Cousin Virginia, since the general and I urged you and yours to seek safer rest, for the present. What we urged then is more true now. Should Sheridan beat Early back, there is no telling where we may stop. You would then be cut off, and in the enemy's lines."

"That is true," the old lady answered, with a cloud upon her face and a yearning glance into the hallway; and a great sigh came, as she added:

"You must be right, Cousin Wirt. I will write to our relatives in Richmond to-morrow."

The veteran took her hand gently in his brown, knotted one.

"You are a brave lady, my kinswoman; and I know your courage. But I consider now that I have your pledge; that you will move within the lines."

The tall crown of her cap nodded forward twice, before she answered. Then her voice shook strangely, as she glanced at the girls and said:

"Yes; for their sake, I will leave Crag-Nest."

The courier rode up, leading the horses. Farewells were said, sadly as though omen of disaster oppressed them all. Val ran to the handsome bay —her gift to Rob—calling his name and stroking the nose he rubbed against her shoulder in old friendly way; and Wythe, on the step called out:

"Oh! major, where is pretty little Santee?"

"I lost her, Miss Dandridge," he answered quietly, turning to arrange his saddle roll.

"Did I not write it, my child?" the colonel exclaimed. "She was shot under him at Gettysburg, as he led a regiment in Hampton's charge."

Why, she herself could not have told, but Val Courtenay felt her cheeks burn red, as she hid them behind the bay's tossing neck.

The colonel and Rob in saddle, and the latter's hand pressed by his cousin for final farewell. Last adieux were spoken; the veteran spurred on and Val turned toward the house. Somehow the major's girth was wrong; and the girl, passing near him, heard the low voice, though his head was turned away:

"Will *you* not bid me God speed?"

"He knows I wish you well!" The answer came from scarcely moving lips; but they added: "For more, ask that *lady* who—"

He was erect; his eyes steadily on hers, his face grave and haughty, as he finished:

"Who is the peer of any in this land!"

And as the low words reached her ear, he had vaulted to saddle, spurring down the path.

CHAPTER IX.

FROM THE OPEQUON.

Dawn of the 19th September broke hot and sultry; heavy clouds curtaining the East, while hot, dry puffs of wind sent dull and low drifts along the crests of the Massanutten, like skirmishers in advance of the line of battle.

But that sultry dawn found the household at Crag-Nest already astir; for its head had at last ceased "thinking about it," and had now determined to move her family—and what of her household goods she might—within the Confederate lines. Answers to her letters had come from Richmond; and, with Mrs. Courtenay decision meant action. Two days had been spent in busy preparation; for the constant clatter of couriers at speed and the rumble of ammunition and wagon trains, along the Winchester pike, all told of early and heavy action at the front.

But the previous night had redoubled all of these; the tramp of heavy masses of infantry sounding continuous; cut sometimes by the rattle of swift moving artillery and again by the rapid trot of cavalry squadrons; while far and near was heard the dull rumble of ambulances of sick and wounded passing to the rear.

And now—the cloud-dulled lances of sunrise still failing to pierce the leaden dawn—low rumbling sounds echoed along the Valley gorges and caught the ears of the anxious women. They were too continuous for thunder; breaking at long intervals, only to reverberate again; and long experience told the listeners that Strategy had once again bidden Valor

"Cry 'havoc!' And let slip the dogs of War."

"It is certainly a battle, aunt; and between us and Winchester, somewhere," Val said, as the three women stood listening upon the lawn in front of the house. "As all is ready, we had better move as soon as the road is clear."

"General Early may drive them before him," the old lady answered, with yearning glance up at the house. "If so, we will still be safe here. And even then, we may be useful to some of the poor, maimed boys sent back from the victory."

"But it may be defeat," Wythe cried, listening intently to the guns—now roaring continuous, and seemingly more near. "Remember, Cousin Wirt said that Sheridan so outnumbered Early."

"Our outnumbered heroes have conquered before, my dear," the old lady answered calmly. "You have not forgotten how Jackson swept them before him down our Valley. But, my children, we will move to-day; because I have promised."

As she spoke, Ezekiel came rapidly toward the house, pick and shovel on shoulder.

"Mis' 'Ginia, I's bin diggin' mos' all nite, an' da grabe's ready."

"The grave! Ezekiel," his mistress answered, surprise dominating her usual calmness. "What in the world do you mean?"

"Da majah ge'en me da wud," the negro answered shrewdly, "da day me an' heem reconloiter dem roads. He say, 'ole man,' sez he, 'when da ladies lebe, you gwine berry all da silver wot 'e can't carry 'long,' sez he. He ge'en me da wud .an' da grabe's ready, an' deep, too."

"Faithful old servant," Mrs. Courtenay cried, "you are indeed a reliance, when our kin are needed elsewhere. And— " she turned warmly to Val—"how thoughtful of the major; so quiet, yet so full of resource."

"Very," the girl answered quietly; "but it seems to me the silver is safe where we threw it in the cellar under old wine boxes and straw."

"Mebbe, missy," the black answered promptly, "but da majah ge'en me da wud 'bout dat, too. He say, 'ole man, look out fur da berry'n'. Da Yank may bun da house,' sez he."

"Oh! He was right!" Wythe cried earnestly. "Burying it is safer."

"Yes; they may burn the house." Mrs. Courtenay's voice shook as it echoed the words; and, for

the first time amid all her trials, the brave old eyes
were full of tears, as she lifted them to the loved
old pile.   But quickly recovering, she turned to
the old negro with the mien of a general conferring
decoration, and to the girls as giving an order to
charge:

"Your fidelity shall be remembered, Ezekiel—
Girls, to the cellar!   We will all aid in the safety of
my husband's silver!"

Promptly all the four sought the dim cellar,
coming up its narrow stair laden with silver, urn
and candelabra; bearing without to the deep pit
in mid corn field.   Then, an old carpet wrapped
over them, the negro packed down the soil, smoothing the surface and strewing blackened stalks
above, to hide its freshness.

Some hours later, all was ready; each sash
and shutter closed, and only the great hall door
still wide, as though regretful to end—even for
a while—its hospitable invitation.   Near it, on the
piazza, the two girls stood with sad faces and
moist eyes; lunch basket, wraps and what bag-
gage there was room for, piled upon the step.   And
Mrs. Courtenay, bonneted and gloved, moved
slowly from one dim and empty room to another,
fixing her eyes yearningly upon every detail of
each, as though to stamp it indelibly upon her
memory.

Meanwhile, the cannonading grew more fitful,

often ceasing wholly for a while, but each time its renewal seemed more clear, and now—as the two girls stood intently listening for the next report—it came so distinctly that the separate guns were noted; and the mountain breeze, now springing up, bore through the gorges of the Massanutten the rattle of musketry, plainly distinguishable.

"Wythe, they are driving us!" Val cried, turning a pale face to her cousin. "God grant I am mistaken! But they are beating our boys back!"

Wythe's face, too, was colorless, but with no fear in the blue eyes as they turned toward the sound, and she answered:

"I fear you are right, Val. God guard those dear to us!"

Still the mistress of the house kept her slow walk through the deserted rooms, deaf to the ominous sounds without; to all save the whisper of that inward voice, ever repeating, dirge-like: "Leaving the old home forever!"

But at last Val's call aroused her from sad daydreaming; for now the old negro was leading up the path from the barn the old mule, harnessed to the old barouche, that was to bear the refugees on their long and tedious journey. And still the cannon boomed nearer but less frequent, while the rattling crash of small arms volleyed nearer and more near. Grave and sad, but calm still, the mistress of the house passed its portals, never daring to trust her eyes one backward glance. But she spoke very calmly and gently:

"It is hard to leave you behind, Ezekiel; but someone must watch the old home, even were there room and were Selim equal to greater load. And you could not leave her—" She turned to the bent old negress who had crept toward the group, her apron over her head; her lank body rocking from side to side, in her race's strongest token of woe. "Good, faithful friends, both! The Great Master will reward you better than your poor mistress can."

With courteous dignity, grand in its gentleness, she took the hard, black hands of man and wife in her slim black gloves. But no further word was spoken when she released them; and Ezekiel began packing the bundles carefully in the vehicle.

Suddenly hoofs sounded on the road beyond. Around the curve dashed a foaming horse, his rider hatless, without arms, bending on his neck and spurring as though for life. With one impulse the girls sped across the field to the fence, screaming after him some query, drowned in the clatter of hoofs. But as they reached the fence another came; soon, another, and then a squad—all reckless, abject, maddened by panic, as they dashed up heedless of query, or answering only by sign.

Pale with suspense—but not with fear—both
women leaned over the fence, straining their eyes
up the road; for the sounds of cannonading had
died away and only scattered firing of small arms
now was heard. And soon another horseman
spurred along, but not so fast; a ghastly stream
welling down his face from the red handkerchief
that bound his head, as he swayed from side to
side in saddle. Val was over the fence and in the
road, screaming as he came:

"What news?"

"Opequon! — Struck our right! — Early de-
stroyed—," the wounded man cried back, but never
drawing rein.

Then came more flying riders, singly and in
groups; many hatless, some coatless, most of them
unarmed; the wretched, ghastly advance guard of
a cavalry rout. But one and all—where panic
let them speak at all—told the same shameful
story of destruction, defeat and rout.

"Val! We must go back to her. We know
all now, and can do no good here." Wythe's face
was very pale, but her voice was clear and brave;
and Val, with never a glance at the oncoming
group, clambered over the fence once more and
they moved rapidly toward the house.

"I know it, my children," Mrs. Courtenay said
calmly, before either could speak. "Sheridan has
beaten us. There will be work for us to do here.

Ezekiel, take the carriage back. For the present, we will remain at home!" ·

The hours of that afternoon dragged themselves along with suspense-clogged feet, for those anxious watchers on the old piazza. They had promptly opened the house, piled their luggage in the hall to be ready for emergency, and made "coffee" for a hasty and meagre lunch. Then, they could only wait and watch for the outcome of that disaster, the extent and consequence of which they could not even conjecture.

But it was plain that they were fortunate in not having left the home shelter; for the Winchester pike—along which their road laid—rapidly grew more crowded with flying squads, first mounted and later on foot; all in mad rush rearward for some unknown point of safety. And later lumbered by some creaking wagons, with supplies or wounded men; their drivers urging their jaded beasts with whip and heel.

The sun having routed and chased away the massed clouds of the morning, now beamed down hotly, half way 'twixt the zenith and his rest, as a great mass of gray jackets hurried round the road's curve almost on the run, confused, half-armed and wholly demoralized. Among them flashed many a red or yellow facing, telling that artillery and cavalry were aiding the rout of the flying infantry; but through and flanking them dashed mounted officers, brandishing their pistols and striving by voice and gesture to shame the panic back to discipline.

Suddenly, out of the ruck one rider spurred across the road, taking the fence and galloping wildly toward the house, pistol in hand; and, ere the others could speak, Wythe Dandridge's face flushed crimson, but her wide, blue eyes never left the wild rider, as she cried:

"Look!—Rob Maury!"

Throwing his horse almost on his haunches at the step, the boy cried:

"Thank God! You are here—not there!" He pointed to the road. "Keep close—be brave! It will soon change! Not a minute to stop! We must turn those curs!"

Little like a boy he looked now; erect and strong in saddle, as Val's pet horse stood statue-like, with heaving flanks. Hatless, his powder-stained and muddy jacket flung wide and the coarse, blue shirt thrown back from the broad, laboring chest, there was the grim set in Rob Maury's features the charge of Torbert's men and the break of his own brigade had left there; and through the firm lips and flashing eyes spoke character before undreamed of, even by the three women hurrying down the steps with eager query.

"Thoburn struck us on the right," he answered rapidly. "Our green men took panic; the veterans could not stand their shock. Can't tell anything of the fight; have ridden miles, trying to rally those sheep! Yes, the battle's over; firing has ceased. If the center and left broke, too, the Luray road below is worse than this!"

"And our friends?" Mrs. Courtenay asked briefly.

"The colonel swept by me like a lion, leading in our old regiment," the soldier answered. "He ordered me to rally the break. Oh! if I could only have ridden at them by him! But I must go; only stopped to warn you all. Good-bye. God bless you all!"

Two women's hands held his; only their grave eyes making mute answer through the mists in them. But the youth's—leaving theirs in yearning wonder—saw Wythe Dandridge hastening from the hall, a huge dipper of water in her hands.

"You must be thirsty," she said softly, holding it up to him, but never lifting her eyes from the ground.

"Oh! Thank you!" Only three trite words; but the color shone bright through the sweat-streaked battle grime on his face, as he took the dipper and drank like a famished animal.

"And take this—*please;*" the little hands held up the package of lunch prepared for their own use; but still the eyes never raised.

"Yes; take it, my son," the old lady said. "God speed and protect you!"

He was gone; crossing the field at a wild gal-

lop, clearing the fence below and plunging through
the woods to head the fugitives now past.

At last the long day of suspense wore toward
its close.

The victor sun slowly withdrew behind the
western hills, and, ready for his nuptials with the
Night, sent hot reflection of his triumph over them
above the leaden clouds, low-lying in the East.
And still waiting, the women sat together;
strangely silent in words, but reading each other's
thoughts as they traveled to the battle-field beyond, and sought to penetrate its clouds for token
of friends, perhaps stretched upon it—suffering or
dead.

Nor did the lessening tumult on the road near
by relieve their unspoken anxiety. Less frequent
squads passed the gate, but these even more demoralized and in rapid flight; and the lull, after
the last of them, was broken by orderly tramp of
cavalry; as heavy force of Thoburn's troopers trotted swiftly by in close pursuit. But suddenly, Val
Courtenay's eyes—turned from the now still and
empty pike—stared steadily toward the woods behind the house; what color was left in her grave
face falling out of it. For, in that very gap in the
old fence—through which Wythe had noted the
absence of Santee, the day Ezekiel rode off with
Major Ravanel—the girl saw an ugly picture sil-
houette itself against the dying sunset.

CHAPTER X.

BEYOND THE LINES.

A man on foot moved slowly through the gap; leading his own horse, and supporting in the saddle of another the tall, swaying form of a wounded comrade. And, the two women, following Val's fixed gaze, all rose without one word and passed down the steps to meet the unbidden but suffering guest, should he prove a friend or foe. But as the pair moved toward them, through the open field, and the light grew more clear, all three hastened forward in a run; but only the eldest spoke:

"Our cousin—badly hurt!"

It was indeed the gallant old Calvert, faint, scarce able to keep his saddle, and held there only by the firm hand of Fraser Ravanel.

"Is he much hurt, sir?"

The old lady's face was very white; but her voice never shook in the query; and before the younger officer could speak, the veteran—braced by the familiar voice—sat up in saddle and answered feebly:

"A hard hit, cousin, but not—" he paused an instant; a spasm of pain crossing his ghastly pale face. Then his teeth closed hard on the gray mus-

tache, as he added—"Zounds! Enough to give
you some trouble with me."

Gentle hands raised to support him on the
other side; and Wythe, without a word, slipped the
bridle from Ravanel's arm and led his tired black,
the brute's intelligence noting the light touch upon
the rein and following like a pet dog. Slowly they
reached the steps; the grim old soldier at once
braced himself to move his numbed feet from the
stirrups. But the younger man spoke quickly and
firmly:

"Steady, sir! Do not move hand or foot. Call
the negro, please." He turned to Val and she flew
toward the kitchen; meeting Ezekiel already running up. With short, strong words of caution and
direction, the Carolinian led the horse close to the
piazza; then, with all their strength, the pair
raised the colonel softly from his seat and bore
him to the broad old sofa in the parlor. Soft, but
experienced hands removed his jacket; by degrees
the high thigh boots yielded to Ravanel's skilled
strength, and the veteran lay pale and motionless,
but breathing easily, as one woman bathed his
fevered forehead, another placed spoonfuls of whis-
key to his lips and the third slowly fanned the
drawn face.

Rapid field surgery had cut away the boot top
and riding pants, and a broad bandage of coarse
cloth was wound about the thigh, hip and side; but

it was soaked with blood and stiffened hard, as Val gently moistened it. And her eyes raised to the other man's in mute query; but he answered promptly:

"No, do not attempt removal. The surgeon was emphatic. Moisten, but do not loose it."

And the wounded soldier—reviving under stimulant—opened his eyes and smiled feebly, as he saw the watchers near; and his faint voice murmured:

"Brave, true women! Always thinking of others." He tried to wave his hand, but it fell back by his side, as he added feebly: "Don't be alarmed—good as two dead men! Pardon the trouble—I give!"

Then exhausted Nature called for relief upon her gentlest soother, Sleep; and—sure that he was resting easy—aunt and niece softly followed Ravanel outside, leaving the younger girl to fan the sleeper.

"How was he hurt, sir?" Mrs. Courtenay asked in anxious whisper.

"Struck in the thigh with a fragment of canister," the soldier replied gravely. "We were forced back slowly for a mile. Then the new men broke and it was a race for miles. At the crossing above he rallied the old regiment, turned it on the pursuers, driving them. Far ahead of his line, he was struck almost from his horse. The

8

men fled in panic; but I—" he hesitated only a
moment—"was fortunate enough to bring him off,
knowing the little cross-roads. Greer, the brigade
surgeon, saw us escape the chase and followed in
the wood. It was providential; or he would have
bled to death on the spot."

The old lady grew whiter and her lips trembled as they whispered:

"An artery severed?"

"A large one, in the thigh," he answered
promptly. "Greer tied it; told the colonel plainly
the danger of motion, and advised surrender for
safety. The colonel sternly refused; said he would
die in preference, and ordered me to mount him
and take him to the rear."

"Will he recover, sir?" The query was cold
and grave, but in firm voice.

"God only knows, ma'am. He has lost much
blood, but has wonderful vitality. He must be
absolutely still; the great danger is hemorrhage.
Greer—if he eluded the pursuit—should be here
soon. He promised to; when he had tended two
desperately wounded officers."

"My cousin shall have every care, Major Ravanel," the matron answered; "and your presence
will—"

"I, madam!" he exclaimed. "Why, I should
not be here now, but aiding to rally and intrench
our shattered force. I must get to saddle at once."

"You must do your duty, sir," Mrs. Courtenay answered gravely. "We will try to do ours, when you go—Wait one minute, please."

She turned softly into the house; and there—for the first time in three years—under the shadow of great calamity and possibly death—the young man and woman were together alone.

"You have put us under great debt of gratitude, Major Ravanel. You have acted like a brave—" imperceptibly almost she hesitated before the word—"soldier."

"I have done my simple duty, Miss Courtenay," he answered low. "You remind me that I neglect it now. One look at our beloved commander, and I must be gone." He turned to the door; pausing suddenly as the clear note of a bugle echoed through the darkness, adding half to himself: "A Yankee bugle—the recall. The pursuit is off."

And he was right. Thoburn's men had followed far and fast; taking prisoners sometimes, vengeance at others, until the scattering fugitives led them through strange roads and into the woods. Then the late chastening hand of the all-seeing Mercy dropped the veil of Night between pursuer and pursued.

Quietly but swiftly the soldier passed to his comrade's side; looking down on the pale, quiet face in the dim candle-light, with his own scarcely less still and placid. Then Mrs. Courtenay came,

bearing with her own hands food and a small de-
canter, as she beckoned him to the door and whispered:

"You must be exhausted, sir. Before you eat,
have some old brandy."

"Thanks," he whispered back. "But I have no
time to eat; and I have not tasted liquor since the
war began. I promised ma; and—" his face hardened strangely—"I have good reason to keep my
pledge."

Again the bugle-note cut the night, now close
beyond upon the road; and Val Courtenay ran in,
exclaiming:

"They are here! I think they halted at the
gate!"

"I must be off then. I *can not* be taken here—
away from the command! Good-bye, ma'am—God
guard you and yours!"

He moved rapidly out as he spoke; pausing on
the step to say:

"Good-bye, Miss Courtenay. If we never meet
again—"

"Quick! They are coming!" as the clank of
arms and tramp of hoofs again sounded at the gate.

Without answer he bent very low to the ground,
his ear turned eagerly toward the barn; and, even
before he spoke, the girl's acute sense caught the
soft footfall of horses in that direction.

"They are there!" he whispered hoarsely.

"They have my horse and I am cut off. I *must not* be taken. Show me the back door; I can escape that way!"

As if in answer, another bugle sounded on the road above; showing another party approaching from that side; and by this time the horsemen from below were nearly at the house.

"I am trapped!" he said quietly but bitterly, as his hand went instinctively to his pistol, "but I *will* not be captured here!"

The girl placed restraining hand upon his arm; her voice very low, but very clear, as she said:

"Major Ravanel, no one can doubt your courage; but one man can not fight the Yankee army. Sometimes strategy is equal to courage. In here —quick!"

As she spoke she turned to the great clock— massive and black in the shadow of the hall; dully ticking what might be his comrade's deathwatch —and swung wide the great door.

"Get in quickly; they are here!" she said again; and Mrs. Courtenay moving to the door, whispered:

"Obey her! Resistance is folly! Remember your country and your mother need you."

Without reply he stepped into the dark, coffin-like recess; and next instant Val stood statue-like by her aunt in the doorway, as a squad of horses halted and faced toward the house. Its burly, yellow-bearded commander and two aids dis-

mounted and ascended the steps; and the former
gruffly asked, with strong accent:

"Vel, who vos dis house belong to?"

"To me, sir," Mrs. Courtenay answered with
stately dignity.

"Oh—ho! Dat vos so? Vel, den, andt who
you vos?"

"A lady, sir," the matron answered with em-
phasis, "as you might learn from many gentlemen
in either army."

"Vel, den, my laty, ve haf got hungry chasen
ter tam Shonnies. Ve vandt someding ter eat."

"And, first, sir, may I ask whom I have the
honor to address?"

"Yah! I haf ter dell you my rang is Macher
Einvasserschwein, commanting der segund reg-
mend von Buford's brigade, andt I be tam hungry,
too."

For one instant the old gentlewoman hesitated,
the blood mounting to the roots of the gray coronet, and her slim hand clinching at the coarse
words. The next, supreme sense of duty to others
controlled her wrath; and her voice was coldly
calm as she answered low:

"Speak lower, please; we have illness in the
house. It is always with regret that I refuse hospitality, even to a stranger; but now I can not give
supper to your men, simply because we have no
food in the house."

"So-o-o! Andt I shall expecdt myselve ter be-leeve dot, ain'd't?" and the man guffawed loudly, as he punched his aid in the side, and added: "Dat vas foine, don'd't?"

"I must insist," rather testily this time, "that you make less noise. My cousin is very ill, and waking suddenly might cause death."

"So-o-o! Your cousin vos eel? Andt who vos her name?"

"*He* is Colonel and Brigade Commander Wirt Calvert of the Confederate Cavalry!" the old lady answered, with all the blood of all the Cabbells rushing to her face. "He fought you, sir, like a brave gentleman, when well. *If* you are a soldier, respect his desperate wound."

As she spoke, again the bugle sounded close and clear, at the turn of the road above; the tramp of a large body of horse coming up to her ear. But the German heard it carelessly, knowing the friendly call; and he drew a step nearer the ladies, as he said:

"Oh—ho! You haf bin hiting ein vounded Shonny, vos et? Haf he bin parole? Tam! Ve veel arresdt heem andt take heem along."

He placed his hand upon his sword and moved as though to enter; but, with swift motion, Val Courtenay stepped before her aunt and grasped the casing, her long, slim arm barring his way.

"You shall not enter!" she said in low, distinct

tone. "If you do not respect this lady's gray hair, you shall respect her home. Three unarmed women are here, nursing a dying soldier. If you be a man, respect our sex and sorrow, and call off your men!"

Abashed for the moment, the man drew back before the fiery tone of the girl's whisper; but, even as he did so, a slight creaking noise, and a dull click caught her ear; and one swift glance showed her the old clock door slightly ajar and the gleam of the candle caught upon the leveled barrel of a pistol, in the darkness behind her. But, even at that supreme moment, she lost no coolness; moving her free hand before the candle in signal toward the clock. For, as she spoke, the bugle on the road sounded the halt; the hoof beats were suddenly still, save those of a detached squad trotting rapidly toward the house.

"Tam! Who vos doze?" the German growled, turning to descend the step; but the squad was upon them, and a stern voice called out of the darkness:

"What troop is this; and who commands it?"

"Troop K, Second Regiment Buford's brigade; Major Einvasserschwein in command," the mounted lieutenant replied.

"Yah! Andt who ter tefil vos you? Some pummers don'd it?" the major growled, and placing his foot in stirrup.

"General Buford and escort," was the curt answer. "Mount, sir! before you report!"

"I vos moundedt, sheneral," the other answered meekly, clambering into the saddle and waving salute in the darkness.

"What are you doing here, sir; off the line of pursuit and without orders?"

"Shust picking up some Shonnies, sheneral—"

"And needlessly insulting unprotected ladies, General Buford," broke in Mrs. Courtenay, with unusual heat.

"Why were we not halted and challenged, sir?" the general asked sternly. "Are these the precautions proper; at night—in the enemy's country?"

"Ve haf known dot bukle vos friendts, sheneral," the other replied, in different tone from that he had used to the ladies.

"Your ears will not always protect you, sir," the brigade commander replied. "Take your command to regimental headquarters at once; report yourself to your colonel under arrest!"

Promptly the German gave the order—not unsheathing his sword; the troop lieutenant ordering:

"Platoon! By the left; trot! March!"

The squadron moved away into the darkness, as the tall cavalry leader threw himself from saddle and muttered under his breath:

"Curse these political appointments! That

fellow may be a first-class ward-boss, but Sheridan himself could never make him a soldier."

"He was keeping a beer-shop in my town when the government honored me by making him my lieutenant," the aid replied, as they turned toward the steps.

"I hope, madam," the general said, raising his hat courteously, "that you have suffered no discomfort at the hands of my men."

"None serious, as yet, sir," the old lady answered gravely, "but your arrival was most—" she hesitated an instant with the word "welcome" upon her lips; changing to—"opportune, sir."

"I am glad for other reasons than duty that I fancied some irregularities here, when I heard horses in your grounds. You have, perhaps, forgotten my former visit, when I was Major Buford?"

"I have not, sir," she answered calmly. "Courtesy like yours then is rare enough among our Northern visitors to be remembered. I told you truly then, that my kinsman was not beneath my roof. He is now here!"

The Federal's face, now in the full light, showed quick change from grave courtesy to surprised alertness. Ere her words were finished, his hand had gone to his sword; and he turned as if to give some order. But, quick as himself, she interpreted the gesture and added:

"He is lying very near death, I fear, General Buford. He can not harm you now."

"I sincerely regret to hear it, madam," the Northern soldier answered promptly. "When we broke Early's right this morning, Colonel Calvert rallied a handful of fugitives and turned on my brigade in the grandest charge of the day! Can I see him, madam? You ladies are alone here; and I may be useful to a gallant enemy."

As Mrs. Courtenay hesitated, Wythe stepped softly from the room and whispered:

"Cousin Wirt is awake, Aunt Virginia, and insists on getting up to see who these men are."

"He must not be excited," the old lady exclaimed. "You had best enter, sir. I am assured that you will be gentle with a helpless foe."

And with no word more, she stood aside and courteously motioned him to proceed.

Colonel Calvert lay pale, unequal to the effort he had made to rise to his elbow. But his eyes were clear and bright as they fell upon the tall form approaching his bedside; and a sad smile moved his mustache as he said feebly:

"You have got me at last, general, where I can neither fight nor run; but the fault is your fellows', not my own."

"I am truly sorry, Colonel Calvert," the younger soldier said in low voice. "I trust it is nothing serious, sir."

Again the sick man smiled grimly as he quoted:

" 'No, 'tis not so deep as a well, nor so wide as a church door; but 'tis enough!' "

A spasm of pain shot across his face and, spite of iron will, the grim, gray mustache quivered as he set his lips.

"Has he had surgical aid?" the general queried hastily.

"Yes; on the field," Val answered impulsively; her great, dark eyes fixed piteously upon the drawn face. "Without it he would have died upon the field. A large artery was severed, the major said."

"The *major!*" the Federal's eyes caught the girl's an instant, then glanced quickly around the room; but she answered calm and unhesitatingly:

"Yes, the officer who brought him here, and escaped your German compatriot."

For sole reply, General Buford turned to Mrs. Courtenay and said:

"I fear Colonel Calvert lacks for skilled treatment, madam. My headquarters are ordered but three miles below. I will send my staff surgeon at once." A grave smile lit his face as he added: "We did the damage, perhaps; so it is our place to mend it."

The colonel's eyes opened calmly and turned upon his visitor, as he said faintly:

"You are very good, general. I shall be better

soon, but I thank you for your consideration for my kinswoman."

"I hope, indeed you will," the Federal answered cheerily, "and you will find Dr. Patterson very skillful." He slipped off his gauntlet and took the colonel's right hand in his, letting his fingers rest carefully on the pulse as he spoke. "We are on the move, but I may find time to call again—with your permission and the ladies'."

"Thank you, general. Come, if your duty permits," the old man answered; and Mrs. Courtenay added:

"If you do, General Buford, you will always be—" again she hesitated an instant—"sure of courteous reception."

With a bow only he passed to the door, followed by his hostess, who asked anxiously:

"Is he desperately hurt, sir?"

"I can not tell, madam," he answered gravely. "He seems seriously hurt, and his pulse is very weak. I should advise stimulants and absolute quiet. Good-night, madam." Next moment he had mounted and was galloping out at the head of his escort.

Then—listening eagerly to the departing hoofs, Val moved quickly to the clock, crying:

"They are gone!—all of them."

Ravanel struck the door open, rather impatiently, uncocking his pistol and slipping it in the holster as he did so. Then he looked full into the girl's eyes and said:

"It is scarcely a fine part I have played in to-night's scenes, Miss Courtenay; but you have placed me under deepest obligation."

"There can be none possible, sir," the girl answered quietly, "when a Southern woman aids a Southern soldier. I had done—"

"As much for any other, chancing here;" he broke in hotly; and the girl, raising neither eyes nor voice, replied promptly:

"Assuredly! You are all fighting for us; we owe you all equal gratitude. I am glad you obeyed my warning. Had you killed that brutal German, a hideous scene must have followed, ending surely in your death."

"And you would have felt—" he began quickly; but—her face still downcast, but flushing as she spoke—the girl as quickly interrupted:

"Deepest sorrow, sir. At this moment the death of every soldier is a loss to the cause—a grief to every Southern woman!"

For a single instant strong feeling glowed upon the man's grave face; with passionate gesture he advanced one step, about to speak. But he controlled the sudden gust of impulse, and the voice was quiet and cold as her own, that said:

"You are right, and your words remind me how I neglect my duty. I must find the remnants of our brigade. God knows who are left—and where they are; and I must search for them on foot, as your German raider carried off our horses."

"You can wait for daylight?" she asked; a relenting in the tone.

"Impossible, Miss Courtenay!" He was entirely himself again; self-contained and speaking in his low voice. "In a tramp after the rout—for now it seems to have been such—night is safer than day, even were time not precious. I know every foot of this country."

"Oh! If you had a horse!" The girl spoke impulsively; but he answered with a quiet smile:

"It will be my own fault if I do not by daylight. So, good-bye, Miss Courtenay; and believe I will not forget your saving me from capture like a straggler or deserter!"

A careful footfall sounded across the field and the soldier's hand went quickly to his holster, as a familiar voice called softly:

"Ez dey all gone, missy?"

"Yes, Ziek; all are gone. Did they trouble you at the barn?"

"I hasn't been at th' barn," the black answered, advancing with a chuckle. "Wen I yeered da Yankee gentlemuns a-comin', I tuk ter da woods."

"It was just as well," Ravanel answered. "You could not have saved the horses."

"I dunno," Ezekiel answered quietly. "Bofe da hosses tuk ter da woods wid me!"

"You brave, smart old fellow!" Ravanel cried in delight. Then he turned to the girl, his face glowing: "What do I not owe to Crag-Nest? Certainty of escape, added to safety from dishonor!"

But Val Courtenay—in revulsion from anxiety—was ice again once more; and it was the cold, reserved voice that answered slowly:

"Safety from dishonor—should be paramount with every Southern soldier!"

CHAPTER XI.

HOME, FAREWELL.

Ten days succeeding the Opequon disaster dragged slowly to the inmates of Crag-Nest. Yet they were far from idle.

True to his promise, General Buford had sent his brigade surgeon over by dawn; and Dr. Patterson's careful examination of the colonel's wounded thigh gave the ladies much hope, yet not unmixed with serious anxiety. The ball had plowed through, tearing the artery; and the doctor's verdict was that the hasty ligation might produce inflammation, and possibly sloughing.

"He has reacted wonderfully, madam," he said to Mrs. Courtenay, after the diagnosis. "His pulse is strong, there is no fever; and, better still, no sort of fear. He seems to have great constitution and to be in perfect health; but the greatest possible care must be taken to keep him quiet. All old soldiers—especially commanders—are hard to control; but Colonel Calvert is so courtly a gentleman that I expect from him implicit obedience to you and his gentle young nurses."

"You and General Buford, sir, have put our household under grave compliment," the old lady

9

said with stately courtesy. "Were all who wear your uniform like you, this terrible war might be a very different one."

"I am more than glad to have been of use," the surgeon replied, quietly ignoring her comment. "I hope I may be able to see him again before we move, but at the rate the enemy is retreating, I may be far out of reach to-night."

"Are there any special directions to leave, doctor?" Val inquired in her thoughtful way.

"None, miss. Generous nourishment, necessary stimulant when the pulse goes down, and the bandage constantly wet with the lotion I left. Only these, and above them all, absolute quiet and perfect rest for the limb. And now, ladies, I must say good-night," and with a bow, the surgeon signaled the sergeant and his escort and was about to mount when he paused and turned back. "By the way, Mrs. Courtenay," he said, "you are now behind our lines; and, I hope, likely to continue so. In this, however, you are not likely to agree with me; and, should you wish to move, you will need permit." He took out his note-book and wrote rapidly, then reading aloud:

"Mrs. Courtenay, of Crag-Nest, with two ladies and a wounded officer, Colonel Wirt Calvert, have permission to pass all posts and pickets of the U. S. Army between their home and the Confederate line. Paroled this 20th Sept., 1863. By order

Brig.-Gen'l Buford, Commanding —th Cavalry
Brigade.

"Patterson, Lt.-Col. Brig. Surgeon."

As he finished, he tore the slip from his book,
tendering it to Mrs. Courtenay; but the old lady
hesitated, drawing herself up to full height, as she
replied:

"But, sir, we have given no parole."

"That is not vital," he replied with a smile. "I
will accept it as constructive. You ladies do not
form a very dangerous body; and the general, of
course, paroled Colonel Calvert."

Never, to her own knowledge, had Mrs. Courtenay wavered from the direct path of strictest ve-
racity; and, in her code of ethics, the suppression
of truth was the meanest suggestion of falsehood.
But the freedom of her kinsman—the comfort, if
not the safety, of her girls—were too great prizes
to be thrown away; so, taking the paper quietly,
she slipped it into the bosom of her dress, even as
she replied:

"My cousin's parole will have to be 'constructive' also. General Buford, sir, made not the re-
motest allusion to it."

The surgeon smiled quietly, as he answered:

"You are a diplomatiste, madam, and I am too
old a soldier to attempt correction of my commander. Keep the paper. It can do the flag no

harm, and may be useful to you. And now, ladies, good-night."

He rode away too rapidly to overhear the old lady's comment:

"That Yankee is a perfect gentleman, Val; and I really believe that I should have been tempted to offer him a glass of wine if—we had one in the house."

From that night the colonel was a model patient; obeying implicitly every direction of his gentle nurses, and gaining strength, and his old-time cheerfulness, under their tender ministrations. Iron constitution and great will power aided these; and a week's time found the veteran apparently well on the road to recovery. But meantime many visitors had wandered to Crag-Nest; some mounted, but the majority on foot; a few of them bearing honorable passport of recent wounds. These last received welcome and care from the lady of the house. But the majority of visitors were stragglers and skulkers from either army—those miserable god-fathers of the modern tramp. And these received small consideration, but always a strong lecture from the staunch old matron, though none of them—if really foot-sore and hungry—were turned away without a crust from the fast lessening stores at Crag-Nest. And the latter could not now be replenished, with communications wholly cut off, and nothing with

which to purchase from the enemy but Confederate
money. So Ezekiel proved himself—in addition to
other valuable accomplishments—a most successful forager; corn and fruit from the ungathered
crop often filling his sack, and occasional *bonnes
bouches* of bacon and canned meats from some distant Yankee camp. These last the girls received
and served without question; certain that the head
of the house would have forbidden further foray
had she suspected their source, or one tithe of the
romance necessary to procure them for the suffering but eloquent man and brother. Meanwhile,
only "rumors of wars," vague and unreliable,
floated in to the cut-off household; but Federal
bummer and Confederate straggler alike agreed
that Early had reorganized his beaten army, and
that Sheridan was massing for a still heavier and
more decisive blow. From Crag-Nest, the only
pickets, patrols and massed bodies of moving
troops now seen were uniformed in blue; and its
women felt, more than ever before, their absolute
isolation. They were, indeed, cut off; and that at
a time when supplies and minor luxuries were
more than ever missed, and when medical skill
might become a vital need at any moment. And
when a week passed by, the quiet of the mending
invalid began to give way to frequent, and sometimes fretful, queries about household needs; but
more especially about the movement of the armies.

And at last, the iteration of the formula, "No reliable news," began to seem to his impatience only the suppression of disastrous tidings. He grew more fretful under imposed restraint; insisted that he was much better, and taxed equally the patience and the resolution of his faithful nurses, in carrying out the surgeon's strong injunction for his absolute quiet.

Then, suddenly through the oppressive but ominous silence in the Valley, broke the dread echo of that order for destruction, which sounded to the very foundations of civilization; hearing which, the Southern Rachel sat by her desolated hearth, groaning in her soul: "Ye have made it a desert!" even while she might not add: "And have called it peace."

Sheridan's order—carrying out the ideas of Lieut.-General Grant—had gone out to destroy all subsistence in the Valley; wheat, corn and stock. Its carrying out had been entrusted to no unwilling hands; and now vast tracts, lately teeming with ungarnered grain, stretched black and bare; while smouldering rafters of mill and barn still sent their curling protests upward against "Man's inhumanity to man." All four-footed things were driven from already depleted farms; and, where not fit for army use, were slaughtered to prevent all usufruct to the stubborn defenders of "Lee's granary." For the fiat had gone forth inexorable —only to be inexorably observed:

"Death is popularly considered the maximum punishment in war, but it is not; reduction to poverty brings prayers for peace more surely and more quickly than does the destruction of human life, as the selfishness of man has demonstrated in more than one great conflict."[*]

And now Ezekiel's foraging was light, while his budget of black tidings was heavy indeed; and, like the ancient, he brought in the latter ever before him, while the former's depleted weight hung behind, woefully light. And—emboldened by immunity from check, from Early's still disorganized command—the black riders of Destruction waxed as bold as fat; and day or night:

"The tramp—the tramp of iron hoofs,
     With mutter hoarse,
Comes on, with flames of burning roofs
     To mark its course.
Far in the distance seen at first,
     The dwellings light;
But, one by one, they nearer burst
     Upon the sight;
And all along that valley fair,
The homeless shriekings of despair
Come throbbing upward thro' the air
     Of pitying night!

"And riding, trooping rank on rank,
With jingling spur and sabre clank,
The men who bear that order stern
Have come to desolate and burn.
O God! May never more return
          A lot so hard to bear!"

[*] General Sheridan's own words.

And now, at last, the resources of the brave women about the sick man's couch had come to their meagrest point. Stimulants were exhausted; nourishing food was not to be had, and the daily needs of all were filled by green corn and parched-potato "coffee"; the fast lessening meal and flour being kept sacred for the sick man. And, only then, the council of three decided that movement —or its alternative, starvation—stared at them as an absolute certainty.

To decide was to act, for the mistress of Crag-Nest. Very calmly she told her patient of so much of the situation as was necessary; that the home resources no longer availed them or him; and showed him General Buford's order for their safety. This had stood them in good stead on more than one occasion of raid or other visit; and the immediate grounds of the home stood almost solitary in immunity. Even Selim had been spared the usual fate of worthless mules; and Eze-kiel had carefully cached the colonel's tall but now lank steed deep in the woods, away from any path.

Told the situation, the veteran bit his mustache and knotted his brows awhile, in deep thought. Then his face cleared up and he said, much in his old manner:

"The order is a hard and cruel one, Cousin Virginia; it is barbarity, not war. That, as I take it, should be conducted much as a duel between gentlemen; and this is the shop-keeper's notion of war. It will cripple us still more, but, as I told you sometime ago, thinkers in the army—from General Lee down—have begun to consider the war a question of time, not one of result. If truly there can be but one ending, perhaps the sooner we reach it the better for humanity and the future. Zounds! Sheridan is helping us to solve the problem. But now for the home department," his rare smile of other days lit his drawn face. "You dear ladies have suffered more than you tell me for my sake. That must cease. Why, I am nearly myself again; see!" he clinched his hand, raising his arm with some vigor, as he rose to the other elbow.

"Cousin Wirt," exclaimed Val, "how dare you? And what sort of a soldier are you, to disobey orders like that?"

"But, my dear child, one must creep before he walks. If you fair tyrants keep me on my back, how will I get strength to ride as your escort into our lines?"

The girl smiled sadly at him, as she strove to answer cheerily:

"The best soldiers obey, without question; but I will tell you that everything is arranged. To-morrow we can start."

"Yes, Cousin Wirt," Wythe cried, overhearing as she entered with some corn bread of her own make. "I am to ride your horse and Val will drive you and Aunt Virginia in the phaeton, until we reach our lines and borrow an ambulance."

Mrs. Courtenay, standing with pale, sad face, moved her lips as though about to speak; but they only moved soundlessly and she turned quickly away, passing slowly from the room. Quietly, but equally quickly, Val followed, slipping her arm within her aunt's and pressing her hand in silent token of sympathy.

"Well, my fair little martinet," they heard the colonel say, "I will obey unquestioning. I have given you my parole. But, zounds! That paper," he added suddenly. "I can not use it. I never gave the Yankee my parole."

"Why, no! How could you?" the little diplomatiste answered. "He never asked it. You can use it, as he said, 'constructively'; and you will not refuse, when it is for *our* safety."

For sole reply the veteran tugged slowly at his mustache. Then he ate his simple lunch thoughtfully, and gallantly kissed the white little hand that reached for the empty plate.

Next noon a negro parson of much reputed sanctity, and more than suspected of being employed as a Federal spy, visited Ezekiel by agreement. That faithful servitor had promised to use the parson in a lay capacity; and, with his assistance, Colonel Calvert—though stoutly protesting his perfect ability to walk—was lifted bodily from his couch to the folded comforter laid entirely across the left side of the old phaeton. Adieux were spoken, as on that previous preparation for flight from the Land of Bondage; but this time the mistress broke down completely, and past the power of speech, when the old negro and his wife kissed her hands, sobbing like little children. Without a word—but with one, long, lingering, piteous look up at her life-long home, she took her seat beside her kinsman; Val taking the reins above the worn old mule. Then the old negro carefully lifted Wythe to Val's old side-saddle; strange-seeming to the fretful war horse.

"Good-bye, faithful old Ezekiel!" the colonel cried suddenly. "We will never forget your care of the ladies. Give me your hand, sir! I have taken a prince's with less pleasure. Zounds! sir, if you are black, you are a perfect gentleman!"

It was over. The home tie was broken at last; and driving slowly and carefully, Val passed into the road, leaving Crag-Nest behind. But not one word was spoken; and neither head was turned for a last, longed-for look.

CHAPTER XII.

HOW BLOOD TOLD.

The drive was necessarily slow, and it was late
afternoon when they reached the first Federal
picket.   Its officer received them gruffly enough
at first; but his manner changed on the presenta-
tion of their permit.

"And you are the rebel officer, sir?" he asked
the colonel.

"I am Colonel Calvert, of the *Confederate* Army,
sir," the colonel answered, as feebly as testily. The
strain of the long drive had told upon him; and
Val, quietly reaching her hand to his, found it dry
and feverish.

"Is there a camp beyond on this road, sir?" she
queried quietly of the Federal.

"Yes, miss; ten or twelve mile, I guess.   Two
squadrons of Buford's Brigade camp there with
his hospital train."

"Do you know the surgeon in charge?" the girl
again asked quickly.

"Old Patterson, I guess," the man answered
carelessly, "and all the staff.   They say the whole
army is falling back on—" he checked himself suddenly, adding: "All right, colonel, you can proceed; your parole is all right."

The old gentleman's face flushed and he seemed about to speak, but controlled himself until they moved forward. Then he exclaimed testily:

"Confound that paper! For the first time in my life, Cousin Virginia, I seem to be sailing under false colors. I gave no parole, and these insolent rascals insist I have."

"But Cousin Wirt, it was merely written constructively."

"Zounds! Madam," he answered, half rising to his elbow, "a parole is delicate point of honor; and in such all must be direct and clear. I brought my sword from the field, buckled about me. Ever since it has laid under my coverlid. It is wrapped in these comforters now. And, zounds! none of these hireling gentlemen ever asked me for it when I could draw it! Why, I refused to surrender when Ravanel urged necessity, after the fellow leaped from his horse in a hail of fire to prevent my falling from mine! Zounds! Madam, would I let my comrade walk through shot and shell to carry me out of their reach when I was bleeding to death, only to surrender now that I am well?"

As his French friends would have said, the veteran was *a cheval* now; and he raised to his elbow with vigorous gesture of his free hand. Mrs. Courtenay did not reply. She only beat up his pillow more comfortably as — the unnatural strength of excitement passing—he fell back upon it. But his mind still ran upon the subject, and presently he said:

"Cousin Virginia, I have determined what I will do. If General Buford, or any officer of my own rank, is at this camp I will explain this business and set this thing straight."

"As you please, cousin," the old lady answered quietly, "but I see no necessity; they will ask no questions."

"Zounds! Madam, I care nothing for their questions! My own self-respect as an officer and a gentleman has been asking questions ever since I heard of this farce!" he cried; and Val, turning at his unwarranted vehemence, noted that a deep flush was on his forehead and cheeks and a restless movement in his eyes. Plainly the fatigue and heat after his long rest had fevered the wounded man; and the quick glance the women exchanged showed that both recognized it. But he was silent now, save for broken exclamations, as he dozed fitfully, but woke at every unusual jolt of the old vehicle. Sunset fell when the picket had been left only about six miles, and its afterglow was fading into dull gray as they passed the next rise.

Colonel Calvert suddenly uttered a sharp exclamation of pain, followed by a deep, long gasp; and both women, turning to him, saw his face deadly pale, but drawn with suffering, and great beads of sweat standing upon his brow.

"Oh! How careless I am!" Val cried, seizing the bottle of lotion and throwing back the light covering from the leg on the improvised litter, stretching beyond the front seat on her left. "I have neglected to moisten his bandage and its **pressure** pains him."

But her own face grew **paler** than his, as a glance showed her the tight cloths, not dry, but soaked with deep red blood, already beginning to ooze through and drip slowly upon the cushion. But the good old Virginian blood that had deserted the **girl's** cheeks had not fled from her brave heart; and, crying to the mule, she dropped the reins and resolutely grasped the bleeding limb with both hands. Passing the left beneath to raise it gently, she felt along above the bandage with her right hand, and pressed it firm and strong upon the course of the great artery. Then, even before Mrs. Courtenay could speak, she cried sharply:

"Wythe! Ride for your life: The hospital camp must be near—straight ahead! Bring a surgeon! Quick!"

"What is it?" Wythe asked; open-eyed at the tone, as she urged the restive war-horse close to the mule.

"The artery! Tell him to bring tourniquet and silk!" Val whispered rapidly, but never turning her head. "Ride fast! 'Tis life or death."

With her words, the younger girl struck her

horse sharply with the switch; he bounded away at full gallop and passed beyond sight in the fading twilight, his rider's light form swaying to his fierce stride.

"Don't trouble—oh-h! You can do—nothing!" the sick soldier murmured faintly, as another fluttering spasm passed his face. But he bit his mustache grimly and took a deep breath, as Mrs. Courtenay bathed his forehead and said gently:

"Cheer up, Cousin Wirt! Your horse is fresh and she will be back soon. It is only a trifle."

What might have been a smile quivered the gray hairs, as his teeth released them; and he answered in half gasps:

"Trifles make up—the sum of life—*or* *death!* Don't trouble—Val—brave—"

Again his eyes closed, as his voice died away in a long sigh; and the matron felt his brow cold and clammy.

But Val Courtenay heard the lessening thud of rapid hoofs die away, with a feeling of despairing desolation weighing on brain and heart. How far it was to the camp she could only guess; some miles at least; and the crimson ooze was slowly spreading over her upper hand, warm and sticky; while it sent great, thick drops trickling upon her lower arm. And with dull, sickening sense she felt her left hand suddenly cramp and the muscles of both arms quiver; and her brain reeled with rapid conjecture of the horse's speed and the lead-like minutes that must pass before succor could arrive. With the thought, she grew dizzy and her eyes closed one instant. The next, she braced herself, body and mind; and, tightening her grasp and pressure, the girl gradually turned herself around; kneeling on the footboard to face her patient and giving the muscles of her back and arms, at the same time, rest and fuller strength.

And still the cruel, red stream oozed slowly through the bandage, creeping up toward her elbow and dropping heavy and dull upon the rug below; and she felt the artery jump and throb beneath her other hand, as though struggling to be free and jet out, at one gush, the dearly-prized life for which she fought. Not one word escaped her tightly pressed lips and clinched teeth. Her quick intuition told her she had grappled with a force beyond her strength; that, in the death struggle with it she must husband every jot of nerve and muscle and will; and—with that calmness which comes to rare natures in the presence of deadly peril—she closed her eyes and forced back calculation of distance and horse's speed, lest thought even might drain the strength so sorely needed.

But her aunt, pale and trembling, softly bathed the now cold forehead—passing an old-time vinaigrette before the quivering nostrils, as she whispered:

"Are you easy, my cousin?"

10

For only answer came a long, shuddering sigh; but the veteran lay still and calm, as the hand the old lady had taken fell limp and nerveless beside him, its pulse barely a thin, flickering thread. But Val felt the artery beneath her hand still pumping piston-like and fierce with every beat of the true old heart; and she pressed down firmer still and braced her heels against the dashboard, as racking pain began to pass up both arms and into her shoulders.

Suddenly the colonel shivered; then drew a deep, quivering breath, holding it with effort as he faltered faintly:

"Don't, child—thanks—trouble—all over soon now—"

Again he was still, as the fast fading dusk deepened into night; and Val—opening her eyes an instant—could scarce distinguish the dim outline of her aunt, bending above the sufferer in the phaeton's shadow. And velvet-shod, but leaden-footed, the minutes dragged themselves along; the two brave women holding their fearful vigil in that thick darkness, unrelieved by even one ray of hope. For, though neither spoke, each felt the other knew how slender the thread on which that precious life was hanging—the pressure of one finger of a weak girl's hand!

Then suddenly the matron whispered, calmly and low out of the darkness:

"Val! he has fainted!"

Still the girl did not speak. Her jaws seemed locked, her lips glued together; a hideous, racking flame shooting from her arms, shrinking her shoulders and searing her very spine! A dull roaring as of distant surf boomed in her ears and throbbed upon her brain. But the marvelous strength of will beat down body and brain, before the inexorable need to bend all power of both to that terrible pressure on the artery.

More minutes passed. At length the cold, shivering dread crept about her heart; beating down all barriers of will and sense and duty to let in the hideous fact. She could not hold out much longer. Minutes seemed hours; and the searing fire in her arms and spine scorched with agony not long to be endured. Clammy moisture thickened on her brow, trickling over her cold face and—as she knew, shudderingly—sapping her strength still more. Louder and faster boomed the surf-sounds on her brain; her throat grew parched and seemed to close; the moisture from her wet hair dropping as from storm-soaked leaves. Thought, quickened by dread, shrieked at her from within that she was human—weak—must fail! Keeping time with the now lessening throbs of the artery, each thump of her laboring heart seemed to jump into her throat, choking and sickening; and she grew dizzy as she saw—through

her closed lids—her own grip relax and great
dazzling spurts of crimson flash by her eyes, bearing in them the remnants of life still left to him!

But the grip of her hands—spasmodic and
mechanical now—closed upon the bleeding thigh
until they buried themselves in the firm muscles.
But—through it all the pure woman's soul never
once lifted itself to the Throne's foot in supplica-
tion. It was a grim death-grapple of nerve and
muscle only with death. She dared not turn one
thought away, for one brief second, from that
fierce, relentless pressure.

She had no time to pray!

Ages—aeons of ages—bore down upon her
through that darkness; numbing brain and heart
and soul—

"How long, O Lord! How long?"

Then, through the black silence crashed a
sound. Horses' hoofs, at a mad gallop, struck the
road above. Nearer they came, clattering along-
side; lanterns swinging high above their riders.

"Here we are! Quick, Martin; the tourniquet!"
Surgeon Patterson cried, throwing his horse upon
his haunches and swinging from saddle. "That's
right; fill that hypodermic, Johnson! Here,
Martin, hold my case and get a suture! Hold the
lantern, madam!"

As he spoke, the surgeon had thrown back the

phaeton's folding top, swung his lantern over the colonel's pallid face and placed firm finger on his pulse. Mrs. Courtenay, deadly pale and breathing laboriously, took the lamp from his hand, as she gasped:

"Is he dead?"

"Bosh! Good as two dead men! Close shave though. Why, miss—"

He never finished the sentence. Val Courtenay opened her eyes one second. The next she had fallen stark and cold across the wheel; only the burly surgeon's quick motion saving its striking her head.

"Lay her on the grass, Johnson! Head low. Quick here! No time to lose. This is a flood!"

He had turned to the colonel again; passing a keen knife under the bandage as he spoke. Its pressure removed, the jetting blood spun high above his head in ruby spray. Next instant the tourniquet was around the thigh; the knife was through the lips of the wound; and the forceps had gripped the ruptured edges of the artery.

"Ah! That's it; now the silk, Martin. Move, Johnson! Yes, the hypodermic; in his left side— quick! There we are! and a d—d close shave!"

Ten minutes later an ambulance clattered up; strong arms lifted the wounded man and laid him gently on the wide mattress. Then the surgeon turned courteously to the ladies—no longer the field-surgeon; the mechanical life-saving automaton:

"My dear Mrs. Courtenay, have no fear. Buford prepared this trap for his own use; so you may be sure it is comfortable. He will be as safe and easy there as under your own roof. By the way, Martin, is there anything in the locker? These ladies probably have not supped. As for you, Miss Courtenay"—he turned to Val, gently taking her hand and pressing the pulse:—"Um! You must take another little nip of that toddy I gave you just now. Don't be alarmed; this is not army brandy, but from my own cellar."

As he spoke he poured a portion in a graduated glass, dropping some aromatic tincture from a phial: "Take that, please! Thank you. And permit me to say, miss, that I am pretty well accustomed to bravery; but you are —a hero!"

The girl's pale face did not change at the words; but her dark eyes gleamed eagerly in the lamplight, as she asked:

"Have you saved him?"

"No, miss; emphatically *I* have not. I have eased him and prevented bad results, I believe. But I am sure—*you* saved him!"

With courteous kindliness he assisted the ladies into the ambulance, passing in a lantern, as he said:

"No, madam; do not fan him. For a man with

that little blood, the night air is cool enough. Miss
Courtenay, wet his lips with this frequently; if he
swallows some it will not kill him, eh?"

"Oh! sir," Val suddenly cried, "where is my
little cousin?"

"Where you will be presently, I hope," he answered smiling. "In bed in my tent, in charge
of a Red Cross nurse. The brave little lady insisted on piloting me; but I knew speed was es-
sential, and she has had ride enough for one night
on that mastodon of the colonel's. Now, ladies,
we must move. He is all right, for the present;
and I will ride by your side. Make yourselves at
home. This ambulance is yours, until you reach
Reb—Confederate lines; and—if Gordon will
countersign that pass I gave—until you reach the
Richmond railroad!"

CHAPTER XIII.

A MORNING'S MISADVENTURES.

Once more the war-dogs are in leash across the devoted Valley; tugging fiercely at restraint and equally eager for the death-grapple.

Time, that stays for no man, has swept warm September aside, and the mellow days of mid-October are basking down upon old Three Top Mountain, where Early has his signal station. That grim old Confederate has massed his troops below and northward; stretching away his advanced line almost to Cedar Creek, where General Wright holds the further bank with Sheridan's advance. For, after his victory on the Opequon, the Federal general had struck but once in force—at Fisher's Hill; and Rosser's disaster at Tom's Run—derisively dubbed the "Woodstock Races" by the victors—was merely an exaggerated skirmish between the now admirable cavalry of the enemy and the demoralized and half-dismounted squadrons of the South.

Why his victory-flushed army—reinforced and splendidly equipped—had not been pushed forward before his own shattered columns could be reorganized and strengthened, the Confederate

could only wonder. He did not comprehend the
vast power of the political upon the military situation, beyond the Potomac; or that popular clamor
was loud, at the North, against Lee's long resistance to Grant's sledge-hammer blows against the
very back door to Richmond. And that fighter—
as well as Mr. Lincoln and Secretary Stanton—
persistently warned "Little Phil" that his next
blow must not be to maim, but to destroy.

The southern situation, still more grave, held
the protection of the Valley—equally the granary
and transportation line, as the bulwark against
that advance on Lee—to mean the salvation of
the Confederate capital.

Early—reinforced by fresh troops, and given
full time to reorganize his beaten veterans—was
now in better condition for defense, or aggression,
than at any moment since his Opequon defeat.
The spirit of his tattered and half-starved men
was better also; new levies, equally with old soldiers of Jackson's Valley wars—being eager to be
loosed upon their successful and arrogant enemy.

During the lull, however, frequent heavy skir-
mishes had taken place between the cavalry, feeling each other's lines; some of them obstinate and
bloody, but all resultless upon the suspenseful situation, until the 13th of October. That day, Kershaw's tough old division struck Torbert's at
Hupp's Hill, driving it in demoralized retreat, and

leaving General Wright in anxious seat at Cedar
Creek.

The opportunity had come at last; and, only the
third dawn, Confederate signal flags on Three Top
flapped out that historic dispatch to Early:

"Be ready to move as soon as I join you, and we
will crush Sheridan.   Longstreet, Lieutenant-
General."

But other eyes than those meant saw the flags;
the spy-stolen code gave its purport to Wright,
and the best mounted courier was soon bearing it
to Sheridan, at Front Royal.   But Early was igno-
rant of this; and equally of the fact that Sheridan
—sending all cavalry but his escort to Wright, and
confident that Longstreet could not make his combination before his return—was speeding away to
Washington for a conference with Mr. Lincoln and
the war secretary.

In war, as in love, "trifles light as air, are con-
firmation strong"; and the Federal general rode
away, while his grim opponent pushed forward.

So it fell out that, at dawn two days later, a
scouting column trotted briskly out of a by-road,
on to the Valley pike.   At its head rode Fraser
Ravanel; three stars upon his collar now.   For his
delay at Crag-Nest, when Ziek saved his horse,
had proved a blessing in disguise, and he had been
just in time to cut off the fugitives of his own brigade that night.   Massing them with some of Cal-

vert's cooler veterans, and ably aided by Rob
Maury, he had turned them upon the over-confi-
dent pursuit; first checking, then driving it back
down the same road, broken and demoralized.
This service had won his transfer and promotion
to lieutenant-colonel of Calvert's old corps, and his
signal gallantry at Fisher's Hill—when his colonel
fell and he held Merritt off Early's rear for hours—
added the third star.

By Colonel Ravanel's side rode Rob Maury; his
collar, too, decorated with an extra bar, for the
youth's good service had gained his step, and he
was now captain and adjutant of his brigade.

"I am glad we heard from the old colonel, yesterday," he was saying, as they trotted on. "By
George! What a constitution he has, to rally so,
after such a bleeding! They were lucky to get
through the very night before Fisher's Hill. And
isn't Val a real heroine, colonel, to act as she did?"

"Your cousin is a brave woman," the senior
answered gravely.

"She's one woman in a thousand," the other
stated warmly. "If the Confederacy holds another like her, and she's young enough, I'll lay my
captaincy at her feet, for better or worse. By the
way, colonel, didn't I understand her to say that
you two had met in Richmond?"

"Yes, three years ago, at Judge Brooke's," was
the quiet answer. "But we are nearing the enemy,

sir; and they must be close enough to keep our
eyes open. Close up the squad and warn the officers!"

Rob rode rearward on that duty; soon returning and riding again beside his commander, as
they turned a curve of the mountain road; descending to more level country—black and burned, with
no obstruction to the view, but muddy and heavy
from recent rain.

"Look!" he cried suddenly, pointing to a distant cabin across fields and far beyond clear view.

"A Yankee trooper's horse, I judge, from the
covered saddle," Colonel Ravanel answered, low-
ering his field glass. "I can not make him out
plainly, but—his rider would not be alone."

"Unless a scout, sir!" Rob exclaimed eagerly.
"He's a find, anyway. Let me cut him out!"

A nod was the reply, and the adjutant—quickly
choosing four men of the best mounted—spurred
at the fragment of fence, the five taking it almost
together, but a tall gray landing just ahead of
Val's pet sorrel.

Next instant Captain Robert Maury was stone-
blind, the morning breeze whistling by his ears,
but sound his only guide, as heavy hoofs slumped
on before and behind him. The field was of rough
furrows, changed to mud by the late rain; and the
gray's heels had hurled two goodly portions of it
full into the open eyes of the squad commander.

Blinded completely—but feeling increased stride
of his own ambitious horse, on seeing the gray pass
—Rob clung with knee and only steadied his sorrel, soothing him by voice and hand. On they
rushed, splashing and floundering here; increas-
ing speed again, as sounder footing offered. And
Rob — fuming inwardly, but too proud to order
slackened speed—heard another horse close behind. Then his own took a ditch in his stride,
speeding away again; and, suddenly he seemed to
mount into the air to tremendous height—to skim
across space for many seconds; then to light again
and rush onward with a cheery snort. In inky
darkness, the rider clung with knee and thigh; but
—not knowing what might be before him—he
dared not loose the rein; and his wrinkled old
gauntlet only smeared the clay more closely over
his smarting optics, as his right hand essayed to
clear them.

Then—after what seemed to him many miles of
furious rush, broken ever and anon by sudden
leaps—a voice ahead cried:

"Ware fence! She's stiff!"

Rob's right gauntlet was between his teeth,
and he quickly drew away his free hand, at the
same moment loosing the rein and throwing the
mud from his eyes with a snap of both hands.
Dimly, he saw the rail fence—uninjured there—
rise stiff and high, ten yards away, barely in time

to grasp the rein and lift the panting horse to the leap.

And on the other side stood the negro cabin, the coveted prize hitched before it, still and quiet. Already the gray's rider had reined up and slung himself from saddle; and Rob's weeping eyes showed him a sorry, low-headed black, covered with an old India-rubber. Saddle and accoutrements, there were none; and the eager hands that tore away the rubber disclosed the hideous sore back of an abandoned cavalry steed.

"Take the rubber, sergeant," he ordered quickly. "He's your prize; and a pretty goose chase we've had!" He turned in saddle, trying to make out his column; but the curving road hid them, and he added:

"We can cut them off by that path ahead. It joins the main pike near Crag-Nest. Mount, men —Forward!"

"That path will bring us in the road a mile ahead of 'em, sir!" the sergeant answered, remounting. "I know the way; escaped a Yankee scout there in August."

It proved he was right, for the squad emerged into the empty pike; no sign of friend or foe visible, though the dull tramp of moving horses came floating over the ravines from up the road. But Maury's quick ear caught another sound, coming from below; and he bent low over his pommel, listening intently.

"Horses; a good party!" he said briefly. "Steady! men—they must be Yanks. None of ours so far down."

Carbines were unslung and ready, and the captain—revolver in hand and sitting like a statue, as the sounds of hoofs each way grew nearer and more clear—saw a Federal scouting squadron approach at rapid trot, the early sun glinting on carbine and vizor.

"Steady, men!" he cried. "Hold your fire! They are far out of range—and too many for us; but we'll give them one volley before we break for our—"

As he spoke, a single red flash shone out from the front of the rapid-moving line of blue; the words stilled abruptly on Maury's lips and he fell back upon his horse's croup, as the bay reared nearly upright, with the sudden tug upon his bit, As he came down, the rider's hand relaxed; and, throwing out his freed head, the horse wheeled round, flying up the pike in mad run.

On sped the line of blue, their fresh horses gaining on the flying squad; their cracking carbines sending bullets whizzing by the fugitives. Closer, clearer beat the hoofs behind; swifter and more near whizzed the bullets, two of them striking with that dull, woody thud that tells of torn flesh.

Rob Maury's spasmodic knee-grip, and his heavy boots, held him in the deep saddle; but—

the chase close upon them—a ball grazed the bay's flank. Swerving at the smart, he slung his inert rider from him, stiff and stark, and falling prone at the roadside.

Ravanel—a mile away around the curve—heard the firing; closing up his ranks, trotting briskly but carefully toward it, his squadrons drawn across the road, carbines at a ready. A brief space, and rounding the curve sped on the wild-flying squad; some wounded, but all panic struck. Next instant the bleeding bay dashed up, nickering piteously; and the soldier's quick glance showed him his prostrate comrade, two hundred yards away, the blue line spurring down, close upon him.

With that glance the Carolinian rose in his stirrups, swinging his sabre high, as he roared:

"Squadron! Aim, fire!"

A quick volley rang out from the front line; the troops nearing rapidly, as the Federals returned it. And again the colonel's voice—no longer soft and low, but with the bugle ring in it—gave the quick commands:

"Cease firing! Draw sabres! Gallop: Charge!"

Spurring ahead, he waved his sabre; and, as a hundred blades flashed out and up, men let out their eagerness in a wild yell, that sent a thousand echoes flying through the hills.

"We'll give them the steel, sir!" Ravanel muttered to the troop captain near him; then, turning in saddle, again he swung his sword, his voice ringing above clank and hoof:

"At 'em, boys! Remember Opequon! Save Maury's body!"

On rushed the opposing horsemen, lessening the gap with every bound; continuous flash of carbine sheering the blue line; the gray firing no shot, as here and there men dropped from saddle.

And now the blue had swung by Rob Maury's prostrate body, shutting it from sight; the lines scarce fifty yards apart, when the Federals swing out, and Ravanel's face—already flushed with ugly fire of the gladiator—suddenly grows pale. Over it sweeps something more fierce and fell than battle passion. The long jaws set hard, as the white teeth close upon the black mustache; the right hand closer grips the long, keen sabre, and the spurs dig fiercer in the black's panting sides, as the eyes, blazing with evil light, fall upon the Federal leader.

Splendidly mounted, sturdy and compact— with heavy brow and dissipated look—the blue-coat rides well and recklessly to the coming fray. But suddenly, his eye, too, takes in the opposing commander, and a deep flush stains his ruddy face an instant, leaving it deadly pale, as his hand mechanically checks his horse. It is but one instant. The next, a black scowl knits his brow,

11

the dogged brutality of the prize ring settling on his face.

And then—the lines almost in contact—Ravanel rises in stirrups and drives full at him.

There is a hideous shock as of two angry waves striking their crests. Huge dust-clouds rise and hang above the rushing squadrons—crash of steel and crunch of hoof; groan of man and scream of wounded beast rising through—as the columns strike each other. Fierce is the melee, as steel hews flesh, and blow and parry and oath make Pandemonium for a while! Then the gray line is forced slowly back, fighting each foot of way.

But in the press and rush, Ravanel is borne past the opponent at whom he aimed; their sabres clashing once as they sweep by. But the Carolinian's is already red, and again a burly trooper tumbles from his steed before it, as spurring from right to left, he nerves his wavering men by voice and mien. They press back the foe steadily and slow; and then—by accident of battle—the leaders meet again.

"Cur! I have found you!" Ravanel mutters through set teeth, as swift turn of his wrist and touch of the opposite spur swing the black half round and the heavy Federal sabre shears down past his shoulder with an ugly "whoo!" But ere it is raised, his own keen point has struck the other's breast, passing clean through until the hilt

grates on his aguilette, and the heavy form, lurching from saddle, almost unseats him, as the blade
snaps close to hilt.

Quickly Ravanel drew his pistol, as the blue-
coats doggedly bore back; the black, bridleless,
bounding forward to the spur. Suddenly a sheet
of flame shot close before his eyes; a deafening
roar, as of a shell exploding in his very face; and
he knew no more!

It was midnight when the Carolinian feebly
opened his eyes, dull and heavy from combined
effect of opiates and a long gashed wound across
his skull. For a moment he was dazed, gazing
dully at familiar faces of his own camp. Then
slowly reaction came, and he made a feeble effort
to rise, as he muttered:

"Did we beat them?"

"Not much," the old surgeon by his side
growled grimly. "We were driving them when
you were hit; and then our boys broke like turkeys.
It was a miracle that Caskie Cullen ever got you
from under their feet and brought you out on
his pommel! But you must be quiet; here, take
this!"

The wounded man lay apathetic, till the surgeon ceased. Then there was a red gleam in the
eyes he opened slowly, as he asked low:

"And their commander?"

"Oh! he's all right," the surgeon answered

grimly.. "If your thrust had not killed him, he must have been trampled to death."

And the sick man, closing his eyes once more, turned his back to the speaker, muttering as though to himself:

"I *knew* I would find him—at last!"

CHAPTER XIV.

THE RIDE WITH SHERIDAN.

The surgeon's account of the skirmish was accurate, as far as it went, but the cause of the Confederate break was not only the fall of their leader, for their front line saw a heavy mass of infantry—warned by the firing—advancing up the road at double quick. This was a full brigade, forced-marching toward Cedar Creek; and with one volley after the flying gray jackets, it reformed, marching straight south. By the time its ambulance corps reached the field, the cavalry bugle had sounded the recall, and the troopers were caring for their wounded. The Southron's sabre was drawn from the body of their dead leader, and it was carefully laid in an ambulance, covered with an overcoat from his saddle. And just then a trooper further off found Rob Maury's body, lying close beneath a boulder by the roadside, wholly untouched by passing hoofs.

"Gosh! The Johnny wore good boots," he cried. "Guess I'll borrow 'um."

He stooped as he spoke, raising the right leg roughly and tugging fiercely at the high, damp boot, when suddenly, to his great surprise, the left leg drew up bending at the knee.

"Darned ef I ever seed a corpse kick before," he cried, starting back: "Hi! doctor!" he called to a surgeon passing, "look at this Johnny, dead as a mackerel and kickin' like a steer."

The man of science approached, leaned over the prostrate Confederate and raised his hand. On release, it fell back like lead, and he answered:

"That blue spot in his forehead means instant death; ball must have penetrated his brain. It must be the contents of your canteen that kicked, Chalmers."

"Wish 'twas," the trooper answered ruefully. "Hain't had no grog to-day. But, doctor, darned ef he didn't kick when I nabbed his boot!"

"Death rigor supervening," the doctor answered with a wise look, as he stooped again, thrusting a rough finger into the small blue hole on his subject's forehead; but the knowing expression changed to a puzzled one, as he muttered:

"Hard substance; ball must have lodged in the bone. He is warm, too; strange case. Here men! Tumble this Rebel into that ambulance; there is plenty of room."

He was promptly obeyed; and the hospital corps turned back, moving slowly north.

It was late at night when Rob Maury opened his eyes feebly. With great effort he raised to his elbow on the rough army cot, staring around him and trying to remember. That he had a splitting headache and horrible nausea, he knew; but where was he? The place seemed familiar; the shape of the long, narrow ward and the high, sashed sides—spite of the shattered panes—reminded him—. Yes, it was the conservatory at Crag-Nest. But how did he get there? Was Wythe Dandridge near by to—. Resistless nausea and dizziness overcame him and he fell back upon the straw pillow.

Shortly after, the surgeon who had first found him passed down the ward, making his report to the chief surgeon:

"Yes, sir, Colonel Clayton's body lies in the parlor there; the two officers are laid out in the hall; the wounded men are in this ward, all except these two." He paused at the very last cot, next to which lay the now insensible Confederate. "This is a bad case; a courier from the rear who rode in here speechless. That gash in his forehead is enough to finish him—singular, doctor, how many head wounds there are in our arm of service; but he had a pistol ball through the lungs that will end him by morning, anyway. Here's another odd case," he turned to Rob's cot taking up his limp hand. "A Rebel officer picked up after the skirmish with a bullet imbedded in the frontal bone. I suppose he is dead by this time. Ought to have died in an hour; but these Johnnies are tough."

The older soldier leaned over the wounded pris-

oner, feeling the penetrated forehead; then carefully taking the pulse:

"He seems to me pretty far from a dead man,
doctor," he said quietly. "The ball may not have
penetrated; simply contused. Queer case; we can
examine him in the morning, and he may walk
about Camp Chase yet." And the pair passed
along the ward, forgetting the two subjects in their
discussion of new ones.

It was past midnight when Rob Maury again
opened his eyes—this time without pain—and
peered curiously into the dim shadows of the improvised ward, trying to recall the strange chances
that brought him back to the familiar spot—yet
so changed! He was still dizzy but felt no wound
or pain; only strange weakness when he sat up in
his cot. So, he lay quietly back, closing his eyes;
and rapidly memory rushed clearly back to the
morning's ride, his chase for the worthless horse,
the approach of the enemy's scout, and the numbing blow that struck him from saddle and left all
after it a blank. That he was a prisoner, he feared,
but he could only conjecture how his capture came
about; whether there had been a battle, in the unknown interval; if Ravanel's party had been taken,
too.

Long he lay dull and inert; even thought an
effort. Then he heard a small body of horse gallop
rapidly up; the challenge of the guard and call for

its officer. Soon "Boots and Saddles" sounded, close followed by "To Horse!" A sergeant clanked down before the ward, recalling the guard, and there was all the orderly haste of a sudden night mount.

Rising to his elbow, Maury stared through the shattered sash-work to the huge bonfire before the house; seeing the men collect from all points, as the bugle again cut the night with clear note of the "Assembly," as the officers conferred in haste. Then it sounded the signal, "March!" and the column filed away, shadowy, into the night beyond; leaving only a few nurses and disabled men about the fire.

The ward lay still as death; the badly hurt men breathing dully under opiates, or too agonized to note aught outside. But a slight movement in the next cot caught Rob's ear; and in the dim light he saw the wounded scout struggling to rise and trying to call. Then, with labored gasps, he spoke:

"Comrade! Quick!—I'm—going—fast! For God's sake dispatch—"

He fell back stiff; and Rob, nerving himself, slipped from his cot and leaned over the sufferer, the night wind cooling his brain. And again, with last effort, the scout spoke—each word a gasp:

"I'm Echols—Sheridan's scout—God's sake— dispatch—jacket lining—take my horse—roan 'Phil'—"

There was a gurgle in his throat. He lay gasping heavily, with wide staring eyes; and Rob mechanically took the clammy hand in his. The scout feebly pressed it, closing his eyes a moment. Then, with great effort, he raised his head—wrapped in blood-soaked bandage, and gasped out:

"General Wright—by day-break to—save army! —ride, comrade—all up with—me—Ah!"

A gush of blood came from his lips, flooding his breast, his head fell back and the jaw dropped.

Echols had died "on duty!"

Still faint and dizzy, strangely weak in legs and back, the Confederate stood for a few seconds as still as the dead man, whose grip still held his hand. But. the chaos of thought quickly took form, as the night wind braced his nerves and a great emergency rose before him. Then — with one cautious glance about the deserted ward and another at the chattering group about the fire—he softly reached for the blue coat and breeches hanging at the dead scout's head.

Stooping in the shadow between the cots, sore of limb and again dizzy with the effort, Rob drew on the clothes, reached for the dead man's boots and pulled them on. The men chanced to be about the same size; and the transformed Rebel, rising carefully, passed his hand across the cold, dropped jaw of the corpse. To his joy, he found the face beardless as his own; and his nerves tingled with a tonic thrill, as his hand went to the breast of his jacket and felt the dispatch crinkle and twist under his touch.

What the paper might be he could not stop to guess. It was from Sheridan to Wright; the dying words: "By daybreak—to save army!" rang in his ears, and he knew *his* general must read it before that hour, and then—. His weakened brain throbbed in his ears at the possibility of what his work might accomplish; and, taking the Federal's broad felt hat, he pulled it low over his own brow. Then, for the first time, Rob Maury felt the soreness of his forehead; the puncture in the skin, that thrilled down his very spine at the touch, and he realized that the shot that stunned him must have been spent by distance and failed to penetrate the bone.

But quick moving thought did not delay him, and he began to turn softly away, buckling the scout's sabre as he moved between the cots.

Suddenly he paused, glanced at his own empty place and turned back, muttering to himself:

"He must escape, not I."

Just then a sufferer beyond groaned piteously, begging for water; and swiftly Rob stooped between the cots, scarce breathing, as great drops of sweat broke out upon his brow. What if he should fail—be recognized as a Rebel! That would mean hanging, for Mosby's reprisals were on every

tongue, and he was in Federal uniform. But that
thought—a mere bagatelle of war's chances—was
swept by that of the dispatch, and his heart grew
cold with fear of failure—that he could not de-
liver it to Gordon in time.

Grasping that precious paper—that salvation
of Wright's army—through the thick cloth, the
boy lay still a few seconds, that seemed hours.
Then the plaintive cry for water ceased, and Rob—
assured that the man had fainted or died—slowly
drew the rough sheet from his own cot; rising to
his knees and bracing every muscle in his still
throbbing back. Softly and slow he slipped both
arms beneath the body of the scout, already growing cold and stiff in death rigor. Then with the
strength of desperation—braced by the grave, unknown meaning of that paper—he raised the
corpse slowly, twisted it about, and—

Suddenly a cannon, clear but distant, sounded
on the night; and the gossipers about the fire arose
with one accord.

Motionless—great beads upon his brow, from
strain on brain and muscle—the boy stood breathless, holding his ghastly burthen. If one man
came in, all was lost! He would swing from a
limb; worse—Gordon would not get the dispatch!

But the men stood listening; speaking low and
nervously, as another distant gun boomed out.
And its dull echo thundered at the boy's strained

sense: "The signal gun for attack! You will be too late!"

With straining arms, molten lead pouring down his spine and muscles of his thighs quivering under their tax, he slowly turned the dead man; laid him softly on his own cot and stretched his own cramped limbs, with a deep breath of relief and thankfulness. Then, as he threw the gray uniform ostentatiously over his bed's head, he slipped the stiff, red bandage from the dead man's brow, putting it around his own. And he was the old Rob Maury once more; for—spite of peril and graver anxiety still to ride away—a smile curved his lips, as he moved off, buckling on the sabre and muttering to himself:

"A grim masquerade; but my head's sorer than his, poor devil!"

The men about the fire stared with some trepidation at the tall figure that strode among them, with clanking sabre and as though dropped from the clouds; but the youth gave no time for query.

"I'm Echols—General Sheridan's scout," he said gruffly. "I'm hurt a little, but all right. Some of you loafers get my horse—a roan; answers to name of 'Phil.' Damn it! Move! I've an important dispatch for General Wright; and no time to lose! Hear that!"

Again the signal gun boomed out for the third

interval and the Southerner's heart jumped, as his trained ear caught the sound of a smoothbore. It was a southern gun from Three Top Mountain!

"I'll git yer horse, comrade," a maimed trooper said. "Yer don't look sort o' peart, ye'self."

And soon he came back, wrestling with the bit of a huge restive roan; high-headed and great-necked, and snapping viciously at his leader.

"Guess ye're too weak to ride this devil," the friendly trooper said. "Yer kin git my mare, comrade; but she ben't fast ez him."

"Better ride my own horse, partner," Rob answered briefly, eying the restive steed and noting holster and saddle pocket unremoved.

He approached the beast that backed, planting his feet and pulling away from approach of a stranger; and a cold chill ran down Rob's aching back, lest detection might ensue. Mechanically his left hand sought the precious dispatch in his jacket; and—nerved by the thought of lost time and what might depend on that paper—all his horse-sense came to him. His right hand grasped the bit, his left hand stroking the corded, tossing neck—then slipping down and gripping the expanded muzzle, as he cried:

"*So-o!* Phil! Steady, boy! Whoa, Phil!"

Next instant he had his mouth against the quivering nostrils, breathing heavily into them; and the Northern trooper stared at the unknown

southern trick, as the horse—whether from bold-
ness of the act or from confident touch—stood still
and docile.

"What time o' night, boys?" Rob asked as he
clambered stiffly to saddle and gathered the reins.

" 'Bout four; two hour ter sun," was the answer. "Ther's ben firin' 'cross you. Guess
Wright's movin' ter hit ther Johnnies by day."

"Shure!" put in another. "Custer's callin' in
every man not bad hurt. Ther foragers wuz roun'
while back, an' cleaned this yere camp. Wright's
a-movin', sure ez shootin'!"

Rob waited for no more. Signal guns from
Three Top, cavalry moving in mass along Wright's
left at Cedar Creek, Sheridan sending dispatch
"to save the army"—these were spur enough to
his intent; and he dug the trooper's sharp ones into
the brute's sides.

Away across field—over the south fence—
through well known wood and dim cross-road,
sped the roan; his huge stride eating space; his
rider more than the Wizard tells:

> "He stayed not for brake, he stopped not for stone;
> He swam the Eske river, where ford there is none!"

But racked by the strain, Rob's head—more
than once in that desperate two-hour race—bent
low to the horse's tense neck, as he reeled in saddle and a red mist swum before his eyes. But each

time, out of that red mist rose the mysterious dispatch; and his closed eyes saw Gordon tearing it open, reading eagerly—then hurling his division at a run down upon Wright's flying columns. And, each time, that thought straightened him up in his seat and the spurs went home again, as his hand clutched the paper and a thrill, as of strong cordial, ran through his veins. But time seemed dragging snail-like, though the cool wind whistled by his ears, and he knew his detour would bring him to the Valley pike, nearer to his goal by many miles.

Then softly the solemn mandate that crowned the Creation had repetition—too familiar to the eye from all time to still the soul in wondering awe. Along the eastern ridges showed pale gleam of gray, brightening and broadening, until The Voice whispered to their crests—"Let there be light!"

The sun had barely given the Massanutten peaks their first gilding when the roan's flying hoofs struck the Valley pike, his nearly exhausted rider still driving spur cruelly home. For plainer to his ear came the dull boom of cannon; signal guns no longer, but in continuous roar of heavy battle.

Who had struck? Who was stricken? Bracing himself in saddle, he pulled the dispatch from his breast, tore it open and read rapidly.

The glow came back to his cheek; the flame to his eye, as he rose in stirrups, waving Sheridan's dispatch aloft, on that lonely road. For it told that the general was far off; that he would reach Wright before Longstreet could combine with Early; and it ordered him to hold Cedar Creek to the last man!

Now, or never! Gordon had the advance; he could be reached soonest. Gordon must have that paper as fast as hoofs e'er foaled could bear it. Knowing Sheridan's plan—but more than all, his absence—the Gray could strike the Blue a blow that yet might sweep him from the Valley! And Rob again gored the roan's flanks, bending over his neck to urge by voice and hand. Then suddenly he turned his ear, listening intently; for over the boom of cannon and crackle of musketry, now plainly heard, the man's scouting instinct caught hoof beats ahead, rapid and regular, but going from him. Half checking his horse, the now worn rider still smiled to himself, as he glanced at his blue uniform; and again he loosed the roan's head and drove the spurs home.

A turn of the road, and straight before him sped a rider on a great black horse, foam-flecked and racing as though for life or death.

With eyes riveted on him, Rob noted the man was short, stout and strong, blue-clad and with some rank marks, and riding as though a Centaur.

12

And, as he took this in, the other turned, gave one sharp look, then beckoned him on, as though recognized—yet never slackening speed.

Thought—lightning-like in peril—told him there was but one road for him; on—ever on, without stop or stay—until Gordon held that dispatch. So, still spurring on, his right hand went out to the saddle holster for the pistol there.

The holster was empty!

But, ere he could utter the oath upon his lips— over the crest ahead poured angry waves of man and horse and cannon; all in one mad rush rearward—panic-struck, intermingled and rushing back resistless! And this on-surging wave— sweeping the road from side to side—tumbling over itself as storm-lashed foam—drew nearer every second.

Checking his black, the rider ahead again waved quick command to Rob, shouting some word unheard through the roar of panic borne on the wind. Then, touching the spur, he jumped the narrow canon to the left and still rode onward through the heavy fields. And Rob—the surging mass of fugitives close upon him—gripped the roan closer and took the leap, behind him.

And both sped through mud and ditch and furrow, the roan closing on the black, as his rider watched with bated breath for the woods-road near and to the right.

But now the foremost horseman slackened speed—bending low to saddle, as listening for distant guns—the roan o'erlapped him.

"Halt! Who are you? Where going?"

The quick words came in deep, commandful roar, the speaker turning a full, bronzed face, heavy-jawed and garnished with long, red-brown mustache. And Rob, checking the roan, felt he knew that face somehow—somewhere—as he answered:

"Courier, sir, from ——"

"From Colonel Edwards, at Winchester. Um! he told me. Ah! You're hit? Much hurt? Never mind that. D—n it, you *must* ride! Keep on to right. I'll find Torbert and rally these turkeys. You must find General Wright, or Crook! Ride for your life, man! Tell them *I* am here!"

"Tell them—?"

"D—n it! are you deaf! Off with you! Tell *them*—tell everybody—Phil Sheridan has come!"

Still speaking, he spurred to left, 'cross-furrows, Rob Maury sitting stunned one instant. Again his hand went to the empty holster; checked midway by that fervid oath, before unuttered.

He had been riding a mile behind Philip Sheridan; had taken orders from his lips; was still in touching distance and—he had no weapon!

Then quick revulsion came. The dispatch might not be vital now, but the news would be grave indeed, that Sheridan was back, rallying the rout!

Again the spur! Again the wild and scarce broken rush; the road above blue with flying Federals, the boom of cannon at the front louder, but less frequent, with every bound. Then came a lull; the mass of fugitives seemed past, while to the left, as far as the eye could reach, the reeling columns halted, cheered and formed, as the great black steed flashed by them—its rider waving his cap!

Straight to right the roan flies, crossing the pike. Close before him lies Cedar Creek, its southern bank gray with rank on rank at swinging run; and the curdling "Rebel yell" cheers him like wine! Into the stream, through it, plunges the roan—clambering up the bank, his now exhausted rider clinging to his mane. Then on again, straight for the lines of the gray; that blueclad rider waving wildly the white cloth stained with Echols' blood.

Hands seize the reins, bayonets bristle at his face; but careless of them, dizzy, faint, he pants:

"Take me to the general!—Great news!—Quick!"

They lead him to a little knoll, where grouped officers sit in serious council; the central horseman tall, lank and grim. His keen, gray eyes seem to pierce the deserter, as he pushes the damp, dark hair back from a great, bold forehead; and the full, stern lips show beneath the gray-streaked mustache and stiff, long beard.

"General, a Yankee deserter! He claims to have news."

"I have, sir;" Rob breaks in feebly. "General Sheridan is in—"

"You're late, fellow!" the stern lips reply gruffly. "We knew yesterday he is in Washington—"

"No, sir! On this field—just ridden to his left for Torbert to rally the—"

"Who are you?" roars the Confederate Commander of the Valley, with many a bounding oath. "How do I know you are not a — — liar, you traitor to your own—"

Reeling in saddle, the other straightens up to salute and answers:

"I am Captain Maury, adjutant-general of Calvert's brigade, sir! Escaped from Yankee hospital last night; rode miles with Sheridan—this horse his scout's—spoke with him—have his message for—Wright—or—— "

An officer caught him as he fell from the roan; the general, gathering his own horse as he roared:

"Sheridan back! — — the old rat! he has walked into the trap, by —— ——!* General, double quick your division and form on Kershaw's right!

---

*Fact. Early's words on learning Sheridan's return.

Harrison, gallop to front and sound the recall along the whole line! Look to the boy! D—— it! he's worth a regiment of scouts! Major, ask General Gordon to hurry all his artillery to the right! Forward, gentlemen! This time, we *will* crush Sheridan!"

CHAPTER XV.

A RICHMOND " STARVATION'S " RESULTS.

"Yes, Cousin Wirt, Coulter Brooke's to have a 'starvation' on Friday, and you are specially invited, if you *can't* walk a polonaise with a grander lady than the Russian Crown Princess!"

And Miss Wythe Dandridge gave the mistress of Crag-Nest a resounding kiss, and just touched her lips to Colonel Calvert's mustache, as she sat by his wheel-chair at the officers' hospital.

The veteran looked all himself again; rosy, fresh and only lacking battle-tan. The gray mustache — longer than ever, but more carefully tended—swept healthy and smooth-shaven cheeks, and the deep eyes danced under shadow of the bushy white brows, with kindly merriment, as he answered:

"I kiss Miss Coulter's dainty hand, Miss Dandridge. But we are not so sure about that polonaise; eh, Cousin Virginia? This old thigh of mine must be all right right now; and I'll try a few steps with Doctor Carter, when he makes his next round."

"You well know, Cousin Wirt, how I would rejoice, were you able to dance," Mrs. Courtenay answered with a grave smile; sighing softly as she added, "or to ride again."

"I'll be a new man by the·time muddy roads permit a spring campaign!" he laughed back. "I told you all, at Crag-Nest, that I was as good as two dead men. Zounds! I'll be better than two old ones, thanks to devotion of my three sweet nurses. Do you know, my cousins,"—his face grew graver and his eyes softened,—"I have not laid my head on that pillow one night since, without grateful memory of Val's wonderful constancy and nerve; and of your brave, dashing ride, you saucy little beauty. Ah! Cousin Virginia, God never made grander women than those with whom He blessed our state!"

"Nor grander men, my kinsman," the old lady replied softly. "Wythe, have you inquired for Major Ravanel this morning?"

"Yes; the matron tells me he is much the same," the girl answered gravely. "He sleeps more; but, when he wakes, the fever rises and he talks constantly. The lady in black never leaves him now, day or night. I wonder who she is!"

"A relative, of course," Mrs. Courtenay replied somewhat stiffly. "I can not tell why her face seems familiar, for I am sure we never met, and she treated me as a perfect stranger when she came to the hospital."

"She's gentle and good to him as his own

mother could be," the girl answered. "What a sad chance *her* illness is, to separate such a mother and son!"

"He will come out all right," Colonel Calvert said cheerily. "These wiry fellows, with calm nerves and iron will, are hard to kill. Zounds! cousin, you never would recognize Ravanel in the reckless devil that charged down at Opequon, scattering the Yankees right and left—literally hewing out a path for me. Yet he was cool as in your drawing room; recollecting every cow-path through those woods. But for him, I had never troubled you dear ladies all these months! But— allons! This is 'piping time of peace,' thanks to the mud. We will forget our stern alarums and dreadful marches for merry meetings and delightful measures."

Truly, as he said, another winter siesta had come, enforced by winter rigor that made roads everywhere impassable for artillery, wagon-trains and aught else but raiding cavalry. So the hostile lines—close enough to each other for pickets to "chaff"; close enough for dwellers in the cities to hear their desultory firing—were able to attempt no formidable movement. Lee's sleepless vigilance—well seconded by that of his generals— foiled graver intent of the raiders at all points; and Early—sore from his late defeat, yet ever watchful and tenacious as a mastiff—was watching

Sheridan's repeated efforts at surprise, in surly calm, from his winter quarters near Waynesboro.

Meanwhile, Richmond was strangely gay, after its own peculiar fashion. Many officers crowded the capital on duty, or leave; and the younger of these—tired and worn from camp—were equally famished for female society and for gaiety and fun of every sort. And the Richmond girls—ever ready to aid and comfort their soldier boys with needle, bandage, lint and equally-prized words of cheer—now seemed quite as ready to aid their plans for mutual pleasure.

In common with their graver elders, these young people realized that the strain was remitted for the moment; possibly they recked that it would renew to-morrow, for the final crush. Yet they seemed content to enjoy the day with all the recklessness of long restraint. Dances were of almost nightly occurrence; not those generously brilliant assemblies which had erst crowned Richmond "queen of hospitality," but joyous gatherings of young people, who danced as though the music of shells had never drowned that of the chance negro fiddler—who laughed and flirted as though there were no to-morrow, with its certain skirmish and its possible blanket for winding-sheet. Many a gallant youth had ridden direct from dance to picket line; ere next noon, to jolt into town on a country cart, stiff and stark—a bul-

let through his heart.   For the soldier boys were
not only those on leave; the lines close to the city
holding many willing to do ten miles each way on
horseback, through snow and slush, for one waltz
with "somebody's darling."

These "starvations," as their name implied, en-
tailed no waste of supplies, vital alike to soldier
and civilian; for a law infrangible as the Me-
dan's limited all refreshments to ample supply of
"Jeems' River" water.   Music was furnished sometimes by ancient negro minstrels, more often by
dainty fingers of some cheery matron; always by
soft voice or merry laugh of "ladyes fayre," for
whom each knight was ready to do—or to die!

The more saturnine, and the more hopeless,
turned eyes ascant, and elevated horrified hands,
at these "starvations;"   but, as Rob Maury had
written to his cousin: "As we fellows do the getting killed, I don't see why the old goodies object
to our dancing in the intervals of the killing; and
I'm coming down to Coulter Brooke's german sure,
unless old Early sends for me for special consul-
tation."

But this winter's siesta was widely different
from that first one, when the mistress of Crag-Nest
had welcomed the —th Cavalry; its rest being fitful—fevered with the hectic of long strain—star-
tled by spectres of foreboding that would not
down for the bidding.   For war, if making all

philosophers, does not change all to Stoics; and there were those who seemed to feel the full weight of the situation; and to look beyond, with no bright vistas intervening.

Val Courtenay was one of these. The girl had grown strangely grave and sad; no flashes of her saucy merriment now answering Wythe's sallies; and when the latter had once exclaimed that she found a single gray strand in her cousin's black hair, the latter had only smiled gravely and answered:

"What matter, Wythe? The only wonder is that more of us are not gray."

But her old-time sweetness and force of character had nowise changed; and Val went about her daily duties—and she made them numerous and all-engrossing—as tried member of that tireless band of veritable Sisters of Mercy, who soothed the pillow of suffering and strengthened the feet that trod the Valley of the Shadow of Death.

While needful, she had watched ceaselessly by the bedside of the soldier she had saved; and still showed devotion to that task in his rapid recuperation, while she broadened her work by visitations to Chimborazo and other hospitals.

One crisp November noon, as the girl was leaving the officers' hospital on one of her charitable missions, an ambulance drove slowly up; and in

the wrecked form of the sufferer from ghastly
camp-fever, she recognized Fraser Ravanel. Stubborn in his ideas of duty—and seeming possessed
of morbid dread of being sent to Richmond—the
young colonel had ignored the surgeon's orders;
had gone on duty with his wound still unhealed,
overexerting his failing strength in the weeks of
sleepless anxiety succeeding Cedar Creek. At
last, mind ceased longer to coerce matter; seeds
of fever sowed in the overworked system stretched
him on a bed of illness, that should have been
grave warning. But still Ravanel resisted; scoff-
ing at sick furlough and dragging himself back to
duty while yet unfit. Resulting relapse gravely
periled a life too valuable to lose; and his general
sent him to Richmond, while still in mid-delirium
of fever. So it was but the wreck of the man she
had said she loved three years before—whom, in
all that interval, she had struggled to convince
herself had ceased to be aught to her—that Val
saw lifted from the van.

Not one of the women who waste usefulness in
hesitance, she made up her mind at once; and—her
face deadly pale, but quiet and resolved—she
sought the matron and told her an officer she knew
seemed desperately ill; that, if she could be of use,
she would assist in nursing him. From that time,
large portion of each day was spent beside the
fever patient's cot; and, ever striving with all her

soul and honor not to listen, could not prevent disjointed expressions from the fevered brain reaching her ears. Nor could all strength of will she
summoned keep the blood from surging to her
brain—or still the flutter of the heart she deemed
so fully schooled—when softer tones murmured of
other days, and spoke her own name through them
all. But one day, moving softly to her post—a
strange calm on her face, reflecting strange peace
in her heart—she stood transfixed; her feet rooted
to the floor and her heart stilled.

Kneeling by her patient's bed was the lissome
form of a woman, clad in black; her arms thrown
about the sufferer's neck, and her soft voice calling his name in that one universal tone, lent by
love alone! For one brief second Val looked. The
next she turned gravely away, moving toward the
door, with head erect, but with that hope which,
unwarned, she had let grow full-statured in her
heart, lying prostrate there, corpse-like.

No word of this she breathed to aunt or cousin;
meeting their comments on the beautiful and devoted stranger with calm, if unmeaning, answers;
and she even went sometimes to Ravanel's bedside
—always in the strange woman's rare absences—
explaining quietly to the matron that demands of
her sick at Chimborazo kept her away. And, in
truth, she was now a tireless nurse; going early
and late, until the colonel warned and her aunt

chided, lest she wear out her strength. But a grave, sad smile was ever her answer to them and to Wythe's loving petulance—that she "never did see such a girl! We might as well be strangers, for all I see of you!"

But through that long week there ever rose in Val Courtenay's mind one query; why her cousin was so gently sympathetic, but so little grieved or anxious, at Ravanel's condition. Spite of will, she constantly asked herself if she could have been mistaken; if Wythe had really cared nothing for the handsome Carolinian, when she cast Rob Maury off so strangely. But ever, after such queries, would follow fierce self-contempt, and angry avowal that she was prying into what did not concern, and had been studiously kept from, her.

But one night, coming in later than usual, and wearied, brain and body with her good work, she found Wythe sitting before the fire, in night apparel, embracing her knees and resting her fair head upon them.

"Val Courtenay! You're just the greatest goose of a girl I ever saw!" Miss Dandridge exclaimed, rising and extending first one little crocheted slipper, and then the other, to the blaze—"wearing yourself to skin and bone and getting crow's feet and gray hairs—for 'duty!' I'm sure you owe some duty to yourself, if not to those who love you! But, you're the dearest old Val, just the same!"

And suddenly—as in their old room at Crag-Nest, after their first quarrel—the younger girl threw her arms about her friend; and, as then, the soft, fair hair was pressed against her bosom. And, as then, again the look of love ineffable—but with more of sadness and maternal tenderness in it—as the tall head bent down once more and the quivering lips pressed soft upon it.

"I tell you, Val," Wythe exclaimed a little later, swinging the little slippers nervously as she sat on the bedside, while her companion disrobed, "so much has happened at the hospital to-day. Colonel Ravanel's fever left him; and, Val, he's just as sane as you are! Doctor Carter let him see Cousin Wirt a moment, and Cousin Virginia and I wheeled him in. They would not let him talk; but he's such a prig for courtesy, he would introduce his sister—"

Val wheeled round upon the speaker, her raised hands holding the masses of black hair that shadowed a face ghastly pale, and the white lips moved soundless as they formed the two words in repetition.

"Yes, she'd been across the lines; business or something. She's so like him; gentle and soft-voiced and says 'ma' just like him."

The other woman still stood staring, the motionless hands not taken from her hair, but the color coming slowly back to her cheek and lip, as she forced herself to say:

"Sister! Why, he told us he was an only child!"

"He never told *me* so," Wythe answered saucily. "He never told *me* anything, except commonplace and tactics. But he is a perfect gentleman, Val; so quietly grateful for kindness, or courtesy. Why, that night of their ball—he *is* a lovely dancer, though!—he took the time any of our boys would have used for flirtation, making me promise not to let our household forget him! Now isn't he a prig?"

The long, nervous hands supporting Val's hair fell before her in soft clasp; the color deepening on neck and bust and arms. For to her sight rose the loved old hall at Crag-Nest, with its antlered rack; a man and a woman contending for a sword beneath it; and accusing conscience scoffed bitterly at her misjudgment, as the man's voice declared that he had perfect faith that Wythe would not forget her pledge.

"And Val, dear, you must get home earlier for to-morrow's 'starvation.' That's why I sent Captain Caskie Cullen off when he brought me from the hospital; and Coulter was sound, as I ran in to kiss her good-night! And Cousin Wirt had—" The crocheted slippers swung nervously and, for

13

some occult reason, the glowing cheek took on a deeper glow, as she stopped abruptly.

"Well, dear, what did Cousin Wirt have, to make an old girl like me go to the dance?"

Val Courtenay was herself once more, but her voice was as soft as the flush on her cheek and the light in her great, dark eyes.

"Oh! nothing *he* had—yes; he had a letter saying your—that the general would arrive in the morning, and that—I believe Captain Maury will be with him!"

"I had a letter from him, too," Val answered quietly. "Dear old Rob! How glad I shall be! You know, Wythe, none of us have seen him since that grand ride, that set the whole Valley shouting his praises!"

"It *was* a brave ride," the other answered dreamily, staring at her slippers.

"But why should that take me to 'starvation,' Wythe? Rob would rather dance with the younger girls; you, for instance. He *is* my pet cousin, but"—the rare old-time smile came to her lips—"as I believe I told you once before, I'm old enough to be his—aunt!"

"And you told *him* so—that night!" Wythe had slipped from the bedside, standing before her cousin, the blue eyes full on the black ones.

"What night, dear?" The black eyes widened a little, in wonder at the tone.

"That night when he—when you—the night that Major Ravanel and I—" Again Wythe paused abruptly, but without a blush.

"Became such good friends that you would dance with scarcely anyone else?" the elder finished for her.

"He danced with you first!" Wythe retorted.

"Only one little turn, dear." Val's face softened and the light in her eyes grew tender at memory of another night; a night under this very roof, when she had heard his pledge to dance with no woman more, until they met; when she had spoken words her lips might unsay, but her heart—never!

"And then you went off with *him*—with Captain Maury; and I heard—"

"Heard *what*, little sister?" The wonder in Val's face conquered reminiscence, as she spoke.

"Of course, it was chance, Val! I know you'd never think me mean enough to listen! I never mentioned it before, because—oh! Val, you *know* I didn't!" And Miss Dandridge, illogical as her sex ever, burst into tears.

"You dear little mystery! Come to your ma!" Val laughed; but a burning flush dyed face and bosom—tinting even the long, graceful arms that clasped her cousin—as she heard her own voice form that last word. But she finished bravely: "Now tell your sister what *is* the matter?"

"It was only chance!" Wythe sobbed. "We

had no idea—Captain Ravanel and I—when we went into the conservatory—that you and Rob—that we'd over—hear you—you refuse him!"

A light broke over the broad brow, bowed above the fair head—the rosy dawn of an idea. Then that light broadened and rippled over the flushed face; and Val Courtenay—releasing the soft, plump burthen from her arms—threw herself upon the bed, buried her face in the pillow, and shook with overmastering emotion.

Wythe stared a moment, her small grief stilled in presence of a burst such as she had never seen Val yield to. Then the plump, white hand touched the soft, heaving shoulder, and she cried plaintively:

"Oh! Val, don't! Please, *please* don't! I didn't mean, dear—I couldn't help it; and I don't care anything—*much*, for him—now!"

Moments passed before the sloping shoulders stilled and the clinched hands released that pillow. Then Val, after what seemed a great struggle, controlled herself sufficiently to rise. Even then, as she turned her hot face upon her companion's wondering one, a strange spasm crossed it and Val's hands pressed hard, commandful on her heaving bosom. But, calming herself, she said with a solemnity that to Wythe seemed truly awful:

"So *you* heard me reject—Rob Maury! Wythe, such confidence must be—" she paused; the strange spasm again distorting her face—"sacred! God bless you, dear—dearest little girl! Never recur to this—until I give you permission. Goodnight, you sweet little goo—!"

She broke off, clasped the bewildered Miss Dandridge in tighter hug, and sprung into bed. And Wythe, lying wakeful in the darkness, was sure she felt the soft form by her once more shaking with emotion.

The next was a busy day, indeed, for all the Brooke household. The general arrived for early breakfast; rotund, jovial and ruddy bearded as of yore, but none the worse for a recent serious wound. With him came Rob Maury—the household hero now, but refusing to be lionized, even when the general told the table that he had applied for *Major* Maury as member of his staff.

But Val managed to slip away alone by noon; and when the whole party called on Colonel Calvert and Ravanel, she had just left the hospital.

Dinner was over and house-clearing for "starvation" done when the girl returned; quiet and with the seal of some great joy upon her face. Wythe sat alone on the wide old settee in the hallway, pretending to read; and laughter floated from the open door of the pantry near, where Coulter Brooke and Rob Maury waged battle royal over a captured pie.

"I'm *so* glad you've come, Val!" Wythe cried,

with a petulant toss of the book. "It's awfully lonely—since the general rode away!"

The other girl sat down, taking the restless little hand in hers; but the knowing smile that just moved her lips left them, as she said gravely:

"I've plenty to tell, dear. To begin, I have seen his—Colonel Ravanel's sister. We met in the matron's room, and she stopped to thank us all for the little we had done for him. Somehow we became sympathetic; and I know her story. Oh! Wythe, she is a brave, true woman, worthy of her race; but she has suffered as few have, for a hasty marriage, against all opposition. Her mother was relentless, disowned her utterly; forbade all mention of her name—even erasing it from the Bible. The husband was worse than any feared; drunken, dishonest, cruel! Finally, he deserted her in Washington and joined the Yankees—three years ago; while I was in this house; and then Colonel Ravanel sent for, and cared tenderly for her since. After Cedar Creek, she heard of the traitor's death; and she rejoices that her brother—whose high pride of name she knows—never met him after his flight!"

"How dreadful!" Wythe exclaimed. "Val, do you know I think it terribly dangerous for any girl to marry!"

"I am afraid it is, some—" the other began; but the battle of the pie surged out of the pantry,

veering toward them; and then Coulter Brooke fled
up the stairs, leaving the new major master of the
sticky spoils.

"Hello! Cousin Val! I captured the commis-
sary stores! Have a bite?"

He advanced flushed and breathless; but Wythe
rose stiffly and stepped into the wide-swung door
of the pantry.

"Sit here, you great boy!" Val answered. "I
want to borrow your memory a moment."

"All right; but I won't lend you my pie!" he
answered, describing a great arc in it with strong
teeth. "Now, commence firing!"

"Rob, you remember the ball we gave to the
regiment? Well, when you and I went into the
conservatory, and you were raging about Captain
Ravanel's devotion to—" His mouth was too full
for speech; but the youth's eyes rolled in piteous
entreaty toward the pantry door. Still Val went
on, even raising her voice—"to our pretty little
cousin, I told you love was a delusion; that I knew,
for I was old enough to be your—aunt!"

"Val! for heaven's sake—" With a huge effort and a huger swallow, Rob got out the hoarse
whisper, his juice-stained hand pointing to the
pantry door, as he rose to his feet. But Val—
blind as deaf to all entreaty—went on, loud and
relentless:

"But, Rob, none of us know anything about

it. You were wiser then—and ever since—in telling me how well you loved—dear little Wythe!"

She, too, rose to her feet; premonitory rustle of impending flight coming through the door, as she placed both firm hands upon the boy's shoulders, and added rapidly:

"Later, in my folly, I said: 'Better one fool than two!' Rob, *I* was the fool, then!"

With sudden movement, she pushed the surprised warrior back into the pantry; and, before she could reach the stair's head, the wild wail floated up to her:

"Oh, Rob! Of course I do. Don't! You've stained my—'starvation' dress!"

But the bright smile it brought to her lips faded from her face before the tender glow of light from within, as Val Courtenay pressed her forehead against the cool pane, and gazed through the fast-coming dusk at the distant hospital.

Then she seated herself at the escritoire, writing rapidly and with firm hand:

"Full confession of fault humiliates only false pride. To *that*, penance; to true regret, it is best solace. In your fever, frequent words made me pity you much—myself far more. Since I met your sister, my sin against you—equally against myself—stands bare before me. If you can forgive it, God will be merciful! And He knows how truly I would expiate it, by lifetime duty to that truth I misjudged so blindly. Contrite for the past—with no false pride for the present—I write what I once bade you call me,

"Always yours,

"Valerie."

Never reading the words, she slipped them in an envelope, sealed and addressed it: "Colonel Fraser Ravanel, Officers' Hospital."

Then she bent her face long upon the white hands, lifting her soul in meekness toward the Throne's foot. And, when she raised it, the last ray of the winter sunset struggled through the shadows and touched her forehead!

CHAPTER XVI.

THE TORCH AT CRAG-NEST.

The soft, warm afterglow of September dusk fell upon the broad piazza, wrapping in its rosy gray the occupants of two ample straw rocking-chairs; but the last, lingering kiss of the day god still flushed the far crest of old Massanutten, as waiting the stealthy creep of Diana to steal it from that hoary, three-headed custodian.

"That new coat of paint warms up, even in this light, Cousin Wirt. Indeed, the home looks almost like the old days once more."

The speaker sighed softly, as the long, white hands fell gently to rest in her moire antique lap; though the sound was not of sorrow, but of full contentment, and her slim slippers crossed in stately comfort, as she added:

"But you are always so thoughtful and so—generous. Pardon me, kinsman, but I fear none of us can well afford luxuries in these days."

"Luxuries! Cousin Virginia, *Mon dieu!* fresh paint is a necessity. And besides, this is not my doing, but Ezekiel's. I only furnished the paint; he gave the talent. You remember the day we last rode away from the dear old place, I told Ziek that he was a perfect gentleman, for all his black skin? Now he looms up as an eminent artist. Zounds! I have seen great paintings in the Paris galleries that gave me less satisfaction as works of art. I was saying so to the general this afternoon!"

A little pause, punctuated by a half sigh. Then the lady said:

"He told me so. He, too, is ever thoughtful. Cousin, in all my years I have never met such a young man!"

"You are right, as ever, Cousin Virginia," came the hearty response. "But for him, you dear women would now be plaiting wreaths for my modest mound, somewhere yonder. Zounds! I remember, as though but yesterday, the ping of that Winchester that tumbled me out of saddle. Your gentle tending—and the girls'—brought me back to life, kinswoman; but he brought me to you!"

"But for him, none of us might be here now," Mrs. Courtenay answered, somewhat dreamily, as the calm eyes peered rather into reminiscence than the dusk beyond. "Ah! kinsman, those were trying days; but with you and the dear children under the roof again, I can forget them—almost."

"Entirely, if you can," he broke in. "When Mars' Robert gave his sword to Grant, six months ago, the war ended for me. I am still a trifle unreconstructed, perhaps, but I strive to look ahead

and not behind me.   There is other work in life
than fighting; and, zounds! the men of Virginia
have plenty of it to do—and her noble women, too!
Voici! Crag-Nest looks like a bride herself; and to-
morrow—"

"Yes; God be thanked for to-morrow!" the
lady broke in—"and for the peace that makes it
possible. Ah! Cousin Wirt, I grow young again in
their happiness.   Hear that!—"

A ringing peal of girlish laughter broke
through the darkening dusk.   A moment later
feet crunched the fresh-raked gravel of the walk,
and a tall, stalwart form strode into view, with a
more shadowy one clinging to his arm.   The
laughter ceased; the tall head seemed to bend
down an instant.   Then silence fell as the pair
rapidly approached and mounted the familiar,
broad steps—creaking now no longer beneath the
firm tread.

"And nothing on your head, my child," Mrs.
Courtenay said mildly.   "Ah! Master Rob, you
will have to learn to take better care of our baby
than this."

"Really, Cousin Virginia, I don't think—" the
youth began.

"Major Maury is excusable, kinswoman," General Calvert finished for him.   "You are too *exige-
ante.*   How can a young gentleman think of any-
body's head, under circumstances which warrant

losing his own? Zounds! my little cousin, in his
boots, I believe I should walk upon my head."

"I'll run in and make Esther light up," Miss
Dandridge replied, somewhat inconsequently. "It
is supper time, and we were just saying we were
both awfully hungry."

"I thought so," the veteran answered quietly;
and as the fair girl tripped into the dim hall, her
cavalier seated himself upon the step, struck a
modern match and applied it to the bowl of a fragrant briar-root pipe.

There was a quiet pause, while the attention
of the trio might have been concentered on the
red-glowing pipe.

The sky behind the mountains whitened suddenly, the cloud edges catching the gleam of molten silver. Then the full disc of the moon popped
suddenly up over old Three-Top, sending her slant
shafts of light full upon the group, and dropping
their reflections broad and clear upon all intervening space.

"I am an awkward cub of a fellow, Cousin Virginia," the young soldier blurted out abruptly. "I
have never once told you how grateful I am. But
God knows I appreciate the blessing He gives me;
and I'll try to prove to you that I deserve it!" He
puffed thoughtfully a moment, sending fragrant,
blue wreaths against the white moonlight.

"I believe you do deserve her, Rob." There was

gentle gravity, but loyal assurance, too, in the
matron's tone. "And you will prove it, my boy,
for the blood of the Cabbells is in your veins."

"And my duty to you is done, sir," the older
soldier added. "My promise to your father is ful-
filled. *Mon dieu!* Nothing can make a man of
you like possession of such a woman!"

For a moment Rob Maury was silent, smoking
with short, nervous puffs. Then he cried bluntly:

"Wasn't I a donkey, though! To think Wythe
was flirting with Ravanel, and make myself miserable—worse than that! to make her so—two whole
years. General, I ought to be reduced to the
ranks!"

"Sentence approved and referred to your new
commanding officer," General Calvert answered
laughingly. But there was a strange softness in
his tone; and he reached out a firm hand, resting
it on the boy's shoulder, as he added:

"You have done credit to your race, sir; for four
long years. A brave gentleman can not be a donkey long, Rob, and you would never have mistaken
had you loved less loyally."

"*He* never makes mistakes!" Master Rob muttered—more to himself than in reply. He jerked
his head toward two others, coming rapidly from
the gate; then hid himself in silence and a dense
cloud of smoke.

"Oh! Aunt Virginia, she will be here at daylight! We walked over to the station and found a telegram, telling us the train broke down at Weldon!"

Valerie Courtenay's voice had the same clear, rich ring as of yore; but the tears had all dried out of it now, replaced by the thrill of full contentment; and the tone was the saucy, girlish one that had charged Rob Maury with desertion on that same spot four years before.

"There was a dispatch for you, too, General Calvert," her companion said, mounting the steps and handing the dingy envelope.

"Thank you, General Ravanel. With your permission, ladies," the veteran said; and rising, as the hall lamp gleamed out bright and clear, he moved toward the door and broke the seal.

"I am more rejoiced than I can tell you, General Ravanel," Mrs. Courtenay said earnestly. "To have my old schoolmate under my roof—after all these years, quite fills the measure of my joy for to-morrow—and your sister, too, general," she added suavely. "As your mother's daughter, she would be welcome, even had Richmond not taught us all to love and know her high womanhood."

"Yes, it would not have been complete without—sister." Valerie hesitated only a second, before the word; but the dark eyes she raised to her lover had in them a depth of love born of grateful memory.

"You both know how I delight to hear you speak so," Ravanel answered in his quiet way—"and to feel that it is deserved. There are no women to me, in all the world, like ma and sister!"

"Say! Cousin Val!" Major Maury whispered, out of his cloud, to the girl—"that's treason. But you'll teach him to talk differently after a while."

"Never doubt it, Rob!" she whispered back, in her old saucy way. "Suppose we begin now. Just offer me your arm for a stroll in the conservatory, and repeat that declaration you made me at the ball and—"

"Hush! Here comes Wythe," he interrupted uneasily. "Don't remind her of what a donkey I made myself; for, in her goodness, she pretends to forget it!"

"Of course she does," Miss Courtenay retorted, in the same low tone—"since you shared with her what was dearer than life; what you refused me!"

He only stared, taking the pipe from his lips; but she went on:

"Didn't I peep over the banisters, that evening of the 'starvation,' and see you divide that precious pie—"

"Bother the pie! *Please* hush!" And the ex-major, C. S. A., jammed his broad shoulders against the pillar and puffed denser clouds than before.

"More good news, kinswoman!" General Cal-

vert cried, coming from the hall with one hand
captured by Wythe's plump little one, and the
other extending the brown dispatch. "General
Buford telegraphs that my letter followed him to
Washington, and he will be down just in time for
the—event."

"He will be welcome, Cousin Wirt," the matron
answered frankly, but gravely. "I had never ex-
pected to ask a Union officer to cross the threshold of Crag-Nest, socially; but respect for the man
—no less than gratitude—makes Mister Buford
welcome, in spite of his uniform."

"Zounds! madam; you don't expect him to wear
it? I tell you that old Frenchman was right: We
know a man when we have fought with him!" the
old soldier cried warmly. "Buford is a true gentleman, as well as a true soldier. I'll risk my
parole, kinswoman, that he comes in *mufti!*"

The lady's face was still grave; but she made
no reply, before Ezekiel appeared in the doorway.
Resplendent in immaculate expanse of collar and
front, that shamed even his halcyon days of the
war, the old black wore a dress coat of startling
length of skirt, and trowsers of amplest width;
both fresh and shining from the tailor's hands.
Under his arm he bore a massive silver waiter; and
there was rejuvenescence in the voice—punctuated
by a stately bow—that announced:

"Da missus' tea am served!"

14

Still silent, Mrs. Courtenay rose, passed her arm into her kinsman's and moved stately to the old dining-room, the younger pairs following with less state.

"Oh! Fraser, how could you?" Valerie whispered, her glance flashing to Ezekiel's new suit.

"He won his spurs, as my aid that day," he answered softly; one of his rare smiles lifting his mustache—"and Sheridan dismounted him, with the rest of us. He will lose enough, in losing his 'young missus' to-morrow, not to have at least the solace of a new uniform."

Very different were the feelings of those seated around that hospitable board now—almost as different was the feast spread upon it—from those days of war. Plenty had not yet spread her fostering wings above the Valley; but, even in those early days the pressure of dire want had ceased to bear so heavily upon its dwellers. And, to those at Crag-Nest, comfort had returned exceptionally soon; and its fruits were never so sweet, as when the mistress of the manor shared them with those about her.

And this was the last family supper, before the tangled threads of Fate would form, for four of them, into that gentle but binding knot, which only the hand of Him who blesses it may loosen forever. But the love that makes the dinner of herbs more savory than the stalled ox was present there;

and the thought of partings, on the morrow—if they came at the moment—only mellowed the joy of present reunion and future hopes.

But at last Mrs. Courtenay said gently:

"To-morrow will be the day of your lives, my children. We must be astir early, to welcome distant friends; and you should have your full 'beauty sleep.' Young gentlemen"—she rose as she spoke —-"I hold it as true Virginian hospitality, as it was Grecian, to 'Welcome the coming, speed the parting guest.' "

A few minutes later Ezekiel held the bits of two horses, champing at the door. Two couples, a little apart on the broad piazza, spoke low farewells; and then sounded the clatter of hoofs, as the young soldiers galloped away through the moonlight to the neighboring farmhouse that furnished their temporary lodgment.

The delicate intuition of the older pair held them in perfunctory discussion of some trifle of to-morrow's decoration; but, when the girls demurely came for their good-night kiss, the fervent lips of the old lady—the grim mustache of the veteran— alike pressed it upon each fair brow with the pure tenderness of a sacrament.

Nowhere are the days of early autumn brighter or more crisp than in the Valley country of Virginia; and this one was ideal in its temperature.

Only fleeciest clouds, here and there, flecked the broad, blue dome, toward which higher peaks seemed to stretch upward longingly through the transparent atmosphere. On the levels, lazy cattle lay ruminant, while from the coverts came the distance-softened whirr of wings, or soft sound of insects.

> " And Nature's voices all accord,
> In song of brook, or pipe of bird,
> To sing, or whisper, one sweet word
> And that is—Peace! "

Noon was well past, and already the sun—rapidly dropping westward from his zenith—began to lengthen the mountain shadows, as memories of the past stretch out to days of life's decline.

The double wedding was over. In the delapidated, rustic church near by, a white-haired bishop, in whose veins also mingled the blood of the Calverts and the Cabbells, had spoken the solemn words that linked four souls "until death do us part." And now his grace sat at the right hand of his hostess, as the family party finished the wedding dinner, in the memory-peopled dining-room. At opposite end of the board, General Calvert presided with a grand dignity, that struggled for supremacy with a joyous *bonhommie* which no feast of all his Parisian experiences had called forth; his especial attentions showered upon the stately, high-bred Carolina dame at his right. Her clear-cut features and still elastic grace of figure might have denied maternity of the younger general, next to her, had not the recent war been fecund of promotions singularly rapid. Opposite sat the pale, delicate and reserved "portrait in little" of her mother, Ruth Ravanel; but the gray strands gleaming through the glossy black of her hair—and the severe simplicity of her black silk gown—hinted at less kindly pressure upon her of Time's omnipresent hand.

But never, of old, had "ladye fayre" craved more courtly cavalier than he who sat beside her; tall, soldierly and bland, in faultless morning-suit, innocent of hint that Pattison Buford had ridden down that Valley by the light of flaming roofs— that the voice, now tuned to society's pitch, had ever thundered "Charge!" upon the very men who tendered now fraternal welcome, with something beyond

> "The stern joy that warriors feel
> In foemen worthy of their steel!"

"That is the worst feature of a country so large as ours," General Buford was saying. "The very magnificence of distances prevents our knowing how charming society may be just beyond us. In my own case now, only the accidental call"—he paused imperceptibly, delicately avoiding even allusion to duty—"business at Washington, made it possible for me to reach here and assist at one of the most grateful occasions of my life."

"I am not sure," Mrs. Courtenay answered suavely, "that there are not compensations in distance—at times in our lives. But, in your case, sir, we are deeply debtors to business for its accident; and I sincerely hope"—she gravely raised her glass with firm hand, as her eye met his with the pretty pride of hospitality—"that you may never again be so near Crag-Nest, without honoring its threshold by crossing it."

"Permit me, General Buford, to join in my kinswoman's wish," the veteran cried, beaming as he raised his glass, "to our guest and—brother soldier!"

Ravanel and Maury raised their glasses—the former's as yet untouched; and that uncompromising daughter of the commonwealth that gave the Union her "First Rebel"—the mistress of Crag-Nest—bent her grand head in courteous sanction of the pledge of peace to "the enemy."

Then Ezekiel moved gravely round the board, placing fresh glasses, of thinnest make, at every place; pausing by his mistress, waiting her command. As he did so, the moving of wheels grated on the gravel without.

"Dearest and best pledge of all must be our last," she said in softened tones. "And time warns that it must be given now. Cousin Wirt, the health of the brides!"

Ezekiel had vanished at a sign from her. Now he reappeared, bearing upon his salver a dim and dusty bottle; its neck resting stiffly upon a folded napkin.

"This Madeira, sent from our kinsman in England," the matron went on, forcing down a tremor in her voice, "was set aside from my wedding day, to be drunk at the first marriage of the next generation. Providence ordained that it should be reserved for these dear children; and I have to thank this faithful servant that it escaped the ravages of the—destroyer of most things, a half-century of time," she finished, with one quick glance at the Federal soldier. "Ezekiel, be very careful."

"No! Permit me, cousin!" General Calvert cried, rising with the elastic bound of a youth, but a courtly bow to Mrs. Ravanel. "On an occasion like this, the Calvert wine should be served by a Calvert!"

With the pride of a connoisseur, but the tenderness of a father handling his first-born, the veteran took the cobwebbed bottle in his sinewy hand. Deftly he inserted the massive corkscrew—never changing the angle of the neck, but bringing out the cork without sound or tremor. Then he passed about the board with stately grace, filling each glass, and standing at his own place with another profound bow to his lady, as he said:

"Cousin Virginia, our glasses are filled!"

Mrs. Courtenay rose gravely, and with her rose each guest. A soft glow was on her cheeks; and her eyes, for once, were downcast and moist. Her lips trembled slightly, but the white, blue-veined hand steadily lifted the brimming glass, as she said:

"My children and friends, our overfull hearts would mock the effort of our lips to speak their feelings. To the brides and grooms! May Our Father keep them to-day and forever!"

In eloquent silence each glass was sipped; two of the toasted bravely radiant with joy—two of them tremulous, with eyes downcast and tear-suffused. But Buford—charmed with the wonderful bouquet of the rare old wine, and sipping it slowly—suddenly noted the pallor of the woman at his side, her face death-like, above the severe black dress. Over the white cheeks rolled two great tears, the long lashes could not restrain; and the bosom beneath its silken restraint seemed rent by a will-repressed sob. Tactful as brave, the Philadelphian glanced across the board, but not before Valerie had slipped her hand into the other's and his quick ear had caught the almost soundless whisper:

"Ruth! Sister!"

The carriage was at the door; the ample, old-time family coach, with age-dimmed cushions, worn paint and massive silver plates, all refreshed so far as Ezekiel's loving veneration and stiffened muscles could compass that feat. Not the sleek and prancing steeds of former times drew it; but two veterans of the war, now translated from squadron or battery, to better bed and rack, wore rather loosely the massive harness of "better days."

But neither vehicle nor team occupied the thoughts of those now grouped upon the broad steps, engrossed in leave-taking; the bridal couples ready for departure for the near station.

The reddening of coming sunset, already in the sky behind the Massanutten peaks, reflected on faces grave and pale—spite of brave efforts of the hearts behind them. The two young girls were close held in the venerable arms of her who had been friend, almoner—mother to them, all those long and trying years. The dark lashes and the blonde alike glistened with tears, that would come; only the eyes of the old lady dry, if filled with yearning tenderness.

"It is hard to send you away, my children, even to your own happiness," Mrs. Courtenay said very gently, as her arms released the twain. "Yet it is but for a little while; and it is not parting, for you will always be present in these rooms. So,

take the old woman's blessing, and go now with
those who have the better claim."

The tender but undimmed eyes turned yearningly toward the hallway—with something in
them like that last look, when they rode away,
after Opequon. But the brave lady forced her
lips to smile, as she added:

"You can not be truants long, you know; for
remember, all your silver saved by Ezekiel, I still
hold here."

"We will be back so soon, Aunt Virginia,"
Valerie said softly—"and we will write *so*
often!"

"And you *must* not feel lonely, auntie!" Wythe
cried, an April smile shining through the mist
in her eyes.

"I will not be lonely," Mrs. Courtenay answered
with quiet voice, but lips that trembled slightly.
"I am wholly happy, my dears, because my children are so. And Sarah Routlege will remain
with her old schoolmate, since my child has robbed
her of hers. And this dear girl, too."

Her arm passed gently about the waist of the
other stately woman, as it had done in those long-
gone days of school-girl love, in the North; and
the other slim hand firmly clasped that of the pale
young widow, whose only answer was a peaceful
smile.

Hearty hand clasps exchanged by the men, and

last adieux spoken, Mrs. Courtenay's arms were about Rob Maury's neck, as she cried:

"My brave boy! I can well trust my baby with you!—and, Fraser, I need not say, what you know!" The stately head bent toward him and her lips pressed the broad forehead of the Carolinian—"God keep you all, my children!"

She turned abruptly, pacing slowly toward the conservatory—alone!

The carriage rolled away, crunching the gravel merrily. After it dashed Ezekiel, with new-found youth and a recklessness scarce consonant with his grand garb. High above his head he waved a venerable shoe, hurling it after the carriage, as he cried:

"Sen' dem luck, Esther!"

And his helpmeet of years—her black cheeks shiny with tears, but her still white teeth glistening with a broad grin—forgot her gorgeous bandana turban and the splendor of flowered Dolly Varden cretonne, as she skurried after him, sailing tiny but worn slippers through the air in heartfelt *"bon voyage!"*

All on the steps stood silent, watching the carriage beyond the turn, as the negroes trotted back from the gate, hand-in-hand. No word was spoken until Mrs. Courtenay slowly turned and, with quiet step, rejoined them. There was suspicious moisture in her eyes now; but her voice was as calm as gentle, when, again passing her arm about her old schoolmate, she said:

"Sarah Routlege, we live our youth over again in our children's happiness!"

"You shame the bravery of us old soldiers, kinswoman!" General Calvert cried bluntly; but tugging at his grim mustache nervously. "You have always been a true Virginian; but now, zounds! you are a Roman!"

"But happily not assisting at a sacrifice," General Buford added graciously. "Mrs. Courtenay, I can not find words to thank you for permitting me to share the joy of valued—friends!"

"The right word, Buford!" the Southern soldier cried, radiant again as he grasped the other's hand. "You and I have seen the torch glow in the Valley. Thank God! We are spared to see the kindling of the torch of Peace—the torch of Hymen!"

THE END.

Society as I Have Foundered It.

By CAD McBALLASTIR.

TRANSLATED FROM THE *ANGLOMANIAC* TONGUE INTO AMERICAN,
BY THE AUTHOR OF "*THE ROCK OR THE RYE.*"

Full-Page Illustrations after Author's Designs.   Price, 25 Cents.

Newark Advertiser: The skit is inimitable in its way.

Portland Argus: There is fun in it, as well as thorns.

San Francisco Call: Written in a bright vein by a humorist of merit.

Toledo Bee: Price, 25 cents; and there is several dollars' worth of amusement in it.

Washington Gazette: Mr. DeLeon's travesties are full of mirth, but his pen is caustic when it takes that line.

Brooklyn Eagle: Humorous in every part, with much dry sarcasm at society.

Mailed (prepaid) to any address, on receipt of price, by

THE GOSSIP PRINTING CO.,

MOBILE, ALA.